THE GOLDEN REVENGE

Which path will YOU take?

Designed by Reuben Barrance
Edited by Sam Taplin

With thanks to Kate Nolan, Simon Tudhope, Tom Mumbray,
Darran Stobbart, Amy Chiu and Lan Cook for their
careful play-testing.

First published in 2024 by Usborne Publishing Limited, 83–85
Saffron Hill, London EC1N 8RT, United Kingdom. usborne.com

Usborne Verlag GmbH, Prüfeninger Str. 20, 93049 Regensburg,
Deutschland, VK Nr. 17560

Cover illustration by Christopher Park

Inside illustrations by Tom Knight

Text, cover illustration and inside illustrations
© Usborne Publishing Limited, 2024

Children should be supervised online. Please follow the internet
safety guidelines at Usborne Quicklinks. Usborne Publishing is
not responsible and does not accept liability for the content
or availability of any website other than its own.

A CIP catalogue record for this book is available from the British Library.

ISBN 978-1-803-70-646-7   8030/1 JFMAMJJASO D/23

Printed in China.

USBORNE
ADVENTURE GAMEBOOKS

THE GOBLIN'S REVENGE

Andy Prentice

Illustrated by Tom Knight

For ninety-three years, the land of Sibele has been ruled by the evil wizard Darkmoon. Protected by sinister sorcery, he ruthlessly crushes anyone who tries to oppose him. Now only a few brave rebels remain, hiding somewhere in the wilderness as he tries to discover their location and wipe them out.

Helping to run the wizard's empire are thousands of creatures who have no choice but to serve him – hobtoads, guard-ghouls, goblins... and one of those goblins is YOU. As a servant in Darkmoon's tower, you're grateful just to survive each day. The only thing that keeps you sane is your best friend Boggo and his terrible jokes. But as you and Boggo begin another day of slaving for your merciless master, something is about to happen that will change your lives forever.

From this point onwards you are in control of an epic adventure. Every choice is yours and your survival depends on the decisions you make. There are battles to fight and picture puzzles to solve as your destiny draws ever nearer and you try to prove that even the most unlikely characters can be heroes...

HOW TO PLAY

This book is split into numbered entries. At the end of most entries, you'll be presented with a choice about what to do next. When you've made your choice, turn to that entry. Your adventure begins at entry 1, but after this it will proceed in the order determined by your choices.

LOG BOOK

Turn to the end of these instruction pages to see your LOG BOOK. This is where you'll keep track of all the relevant details of your quest. It's split into the five sections detailed below, and you'll need a pencil to keep them all up to date.

Life points

You start with 12 LIFE points, but lose points if you're hurt. If you drop to 0 you die, and the game ends. At various points you'll be able to heal yourself and regain lost LIFE points, **but you can never have more than 12 in total**. Each time you gain or lose LIFE points, update the number in your LOG BOOK.

Abilities

You have three abilities: STRENGTH, SNEAK and WITS. Your starting level for each is 1 point. Before you start the game, add 1 point to the ability of your choice. At various moments in your quest, you will gain more ability points. It's up to you which abilities to upgrade. If you receive more than 1 ability point at the same time, you can add them all to the same ability, or spread them across different abilities. You can also lose ability points, and you must decide which ability to downgrade. Remember to update your LOG BOOK whenever an ability level changes.

Items and Weapons

You will both pick up and lose items on your adventure. Remember to write down any item that you pick up in your LOG BOOK, and delete it if you're instructed to do so. Most items can help you in some way. Some items are weapons. **Until you have a weapon you will have to subtract 1 from your total when you roll your dice in combat because you are unarmed.** When you pick up a weapon, write it down in your LOG BOOK. If the weapon has a special ability, make a note of it in the same box.

Notes

During your quest, you'll see and learn things that could be useful later on. It might be a small detail, or an entry number you want to refer back to. You can jot these down in the notes section of your LOG BOOK.

RING CHECKS

Your RING SCORE starts at 0. At various points during your adventure you will be asked to roll a ring check. Before every ring check add 1 point to your RING SCORE by filling in a section on your Ring Tracker, then roll one dice and compare the result to your new RING SCORE. If the number rolled is higher than your RING SCORE you pass the ring check. If the number rolled is equal to or lower than your RING SCORE you fail the ring check. Remember to record your new RING SCORE **before** you roll the ring check.

COMBAT

You fight by rolling two dice. Here's an example of what you'll see before combat starts:

GUARD

Rounds: 5   Damage: 2

YOU

The skulls are your opponent's Combat points. The aim is to cross them all out, and you must do this within a certain number of rounds. One skull is one Combat point. The number of rounds you have to defeat your opponent is shown to the left beneath their name.

At the start of each round, you decide how strong an attack to launch against your opponent. You have two options:

Standard attack

Roll 7 or more: your opponent loses 1 Combat point

Power attack

Roll 9 or more: your opponent loses 3 Combat points

Once you've chosen, roll two dice. Remember, if you choose to roll for '7 or more' but actually roll a 10, you still only score the points for '7 or more'.

If you go for a Power attack, your chances of success are lower – but you only have a limited number of rounds in which to cross out all your opponent's Combat points. If you fail to do so, you must turn to the Defeat entry. Remember, defeat does not necessarily mean death. Every time you fail to match your chosen roll, you must cross out one or more of your Life points. These are the hearts beneath your heading. One heart is one Life point. To find out how many to cross out, look at your opponent's Damage rating, which is shown to the right beneath their name. If your Life points are reduced to zero at any point in the combat, you are dead and your adventure is over.

Before the fight starts, check your Log Book to see how many Life points you have. Then turn back to the combat entry, and cross out any hearts needed to show the correct amount. Once the fight is over, update your Log Book if you lost any Life points.

If you're fighting more than one opponent, you must choose which opponent you want to attack before every roll. You don't have to defeat one opponent before moving on to the next, but you must defeat all your opponents before turning to the Victory entry.

For a step-by-step example of how combat works, turn to the back of the book.

PICTURE PUZZLES

There are eleven picture puzzles, but which ones you encounter will depend on the choices you make on your journey. If you solve a puzzle correctly, it will reveal an entry number to turn to. If you can't solve the puzzle, you'll be given a different entry number. But don't give up too soon, or your quest could come to an unhappy end.

Read the text that leads into the puzzle closely – often there will be clues there to help you. And remember that you won't always be able to solve the puzzle simply by looking at the picture. Sometimes you might have to move the page around to reveal the answer...

USBORNE QUICKLINKS

If you don't have two dice for the combat, you can use an online dice roller instead. For links to websites with dice rollers, and extra copies of the Log Book to print out, go to usborne.com/Quicklinks and enter 'Goblin's Revenge', or simply scan the QR code below.

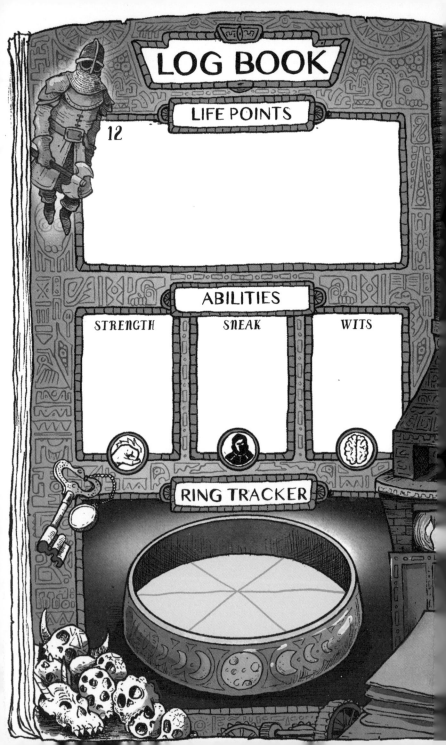

LOG BOOK

LIFE POINTS

12

ABILITIES

STRENGTH

SNEAK

WITS

RING TRACKER

ITEMS

NOTES

"Do you really think the Master's spell will find the rebels?" asks Boggo. "His other spells haven't..."

You're too busy hauling the heavy cauldron of dragon blood up the stairs to worry about a spell. There are many stairs in the Black Tower, and Darkmoon's chambers are at the very top.

"Can't you just concentrate?" you hiss. "We're nearly there." Your arms are aching because Boggo is not pulling his weight – but then he never does. For some reason his laziness has never stopped him being your best friend. Probably because he's the most cheerful goblin you've ever met.

The Master's door is open and you clump into his chamber together, hampered by the cauldron banging against your ankles. The Master is staring hard at his magic mirror. Thick pipes run from the mirror to the rune engine, which is waiting for the blood you've carried up from the dungeons.

"Too slow, goblins. Fill it up." Darkmoon doesn't look away from the mirror. Together, you carefully funnel the blood from the cauldron into the engine. A little spatters on the floor but the rest flows into the device, which starts to hum. As usual, Boggo isn't paying attention: he's staring, fascinated, at Darkmoon and the large oval mirror, where a dim shape has just started to shimmer up from the depths.

"Yes... yes! Now at last I sniff out those rebel rats!" mutters Darkmoon. But just as he speaks, the engine's hum comes to a shuddering stop and the shape in the mirror vanishes. "NO! Not yet! Not enough power," Darkmoon hisses. "I need MORE!"

He glances at you and Boggo. "Hmm. Yes. You'll do nicely." Then he points and clicks his fingers. You flinch away, but Boggo is lifted into the air. He shouts with surprise as a tendril of pale fire ripples between his floating body and the rune engine. The device hums to life at once and the glowing shape reappears inside the magic mirror.

Boggo's lifeless body thumps to the floor. The Master cackles with delight as the shape in the mirror shivers into focus.

"Now! Now I've found you!" he shouts. He's not bothered that he's just murdered your best friend – he might as well have squashed a fly. All his attention is on the mirror, which now shows a view of a misty waterfall that rushes out of a dark cave and tumbles down a cliff. A ruined fortress squats on the mountaintop above it.

"So that's where they've dug their hole!" he whispers. "At Crow Cave! In the caverns beneath the castle. I should have guessed..." He throws his head back and cackles again.

You should be afraid. You should be sad. But somehow, you're not. Most of all you're angry. Boggo is dead. And for what? You slink away. You're good at that. You know exactly where you're going – straight to the shelf where the Master stores his greatest treasures. You and Boggo have dusted that shelf a hundred times. You ignore the Orb of Damnation, the Folded Star and the Sceptre of Truth. You know what the Master loves most, and you take it.

Add the NIGHT RING to your LOG BOOK as you remove it from the shelf.

Darkmoon, wrapped up in gloating triumph, takes no notice. That's not unusual – no one ever notices a goblin. You trot towards the door, slipping the heavy iron ring into your waistcoat pocket. As you leave the room, a magical alarm begins to wail and you run for your life.

To take the fastest route out of the castle through the gatehouse, turn to **68**.

To take the back stairs down to the kitchen, turn to **324**.

2

As you follow the winding path between the trees, you have a prickly feeling on the back of your neck as if you're being watched – but you don't actually see the tree dragon. The forest is dim and quiet and seems to go on forever, with patches of bright flowers scattered here and there. You stop at a stream and have a drink. It's delicious and refreshing, and you dunk your head in the cool water. When you lift it out, dripping, you get a nasty surprise: there's a wolf right beside you. It's snarling, and it looks hungry. Its muscles are tensed to pounce.

To try to attack the wolf before it attacks you, turn to **17**.

To back away from the wolf, turn to **216**.

3

You approach them slowly and openly, walking up the middle of the road. There are five humans, two parents you think, with three small children. You can see they've been trying to light a fire with damp wood and it hasn't worked. One of the children sees you coming and yelps in alarm, then the father jumps into your path, brandishing a staff.

"No closer, goblin!" he shouts.

"I just want to help," you say, holding up your hands palm out. "I mean no harm to your family."

If you have a FLASK OF OIL or a TINDERBOX, turn to **79**.

Otherwise, roll one dice and add it to your WITS level.

If your total is 7 or higher, turn to **143**.

If your total is 6 or lower, turn to **103**.

4

You get up on tiptoes and peer over the balcony: a series of stepped roofs like a giant's staircase falls away beneath you. You might be able to jump down to the nearest roof, though it's quite a long way. Another plan might be to pull out some of the tubes that are connected to the plant pots and use those as a rope to climb down from the balcony instead. The plants rustle softly as you ponder what to do.

To use the tubes as a rope, turn to **154**.

To jump, turn to **238**.

If you have the WOODEN WHISTLE and would like to blow it, turn to **15**.

5

"Now you must unleash the waterfall," says the Iron Smith. *"You cannot fire the forge without the cooling power of water. Go to the far wall and release the stream."*

You pick your way across the floor, using small bridges to cross the channels that now run with glowing lava. The air is filling with smoke now, and it's a lot warmer. The wall is covered in scaffolding and you look up into it, grateful for the cooling drops of water that drip from the complex system of chutes and gates and smaller wheels that in turn support the big waterwheel high above. Glowmoss has thrived in the damp and its gleam casts bright light over the huge mechanism.

In front of you there's a single giant lever, and you pull it. A trapdoor opens in the ceiling and a cascade of water drops through the chamber, landing directly on the great wheel in a violent burst of spray and mist. As the gears begin to grind and grumble, the wheel starts to turn and water flows through the system, rolling down chutes and pipes. But suddenly a wild torrent splashes down from somewhere in the middle, drenching you completely.

"*Something is not functioning as it should,*" says the Smith. "*There is a blockage. You must fix it.*"

Roll one dice and add it to your WITS level.

If your total is 8 or higher, turn to **38**.

If your total is 7 or lower, turn to **303**.

6

You know you've been found, but still you try to escape. But you're only five minutes downriver when you hear a chuckle overhead. Marcox, the Master's butler, is hovering just above you.

"Thank you so much for using the ring," he sneers. "It made it exceedingly easy to find you."

The ring! You reach for your pocket, but your hand never makes it. With a dismissive gesture, Marcox freezes you in place. He floats down to the boat and lands softly beside you. You watch, powerless, as he pulls the ring from your pocket and waves his hand towards you. Everything goes black. Soon your lifeless body is floating down the river in the boat.

7

You climb over the giant tree trunk as carefully as you can, but your foot slips on a patch of moss and your fingers touch the rot. You snatch them away, but not before its poison has seeped into your skin. Your hand begins to blister and sting.

Deduct 1 LIFE point and turn to **188**.

8

You reach for the platter of fried beetle.

"You thieving goblin!" roars an angry voice. A large palm, belonging to someone you don't see, smacks you hard around the ear. You go flying across the kitchen and smash into a basket of fish guts, which empties all over you. Stinking of fish and with your ears ringing, you stumble to your feet. To your relief, Midge waves you over and you hurry across to her.

Deduct 1 LIFE point and turn to **28**.

9

You slip down a last alley and emerge into a narrow street lined with rundown buildings.

"*That's the one,*" says Boggo, pointing. His parents' house is a fisherman's shack leaning out over the river. You tiptoe up to the window and see a couple of old goblins sitting down to their dinner. From the smell, they're having crab chowder. You crouch down in the shadows while Boggo peers in. There's no glass in the window, so you hear everything that's being said.

"What d'you reckon the raid's about this time?" says the old lady, cracking a crab's claw between her teeth.

"*Hi Mum,*" whispers Boggo.

"Darkmoon jus' can't let an honest goblin alone," growls the old man.

"*Hi Dad,*" whispers Boggo.

"You ain't never been honest though, has you Fred?" cackles Boggo's mum. "Here, have some more soup you old rascal."

"*Goodbye.*" There's a catch in Boggo's voice and you glance up. Ghostly tears are streaming down his cheeks. The shouts of the soldiers are very close now – they're in the next street.

"*Thanks friend,*" says Boggo. "*I've seen 'em now. Time to get out of here.*" He wipes his eyes, and you see the uncertainty in his face – the request he's left unspoken.

"Do you want me to tell them you're dead?" you say.

"Y...no!" he says. "*It'd break their hearts – and it's too dangerous. You need to get off the streets. You can get a boat from the jetty over there, and hit the river.*"

Staying any longer would be a big risk, but you can tell he wants his parents to know what's happened to him.

To try and escape the village immediately, turn to **261**.

To try to talk to Boggo's parents, turn to **141**.

"I don't know!" you blurt out. "The alarm just started ringing. I was on my way down."

"Pah! Useless goblin," spits Marcox, turning away from you and striding up the stairs with his guards. It's a huge relief when he's gone – though you still feel as though his black eyes are burning into you. You know this is no time to relax: there'll be more guards soon and it's still a long way to the bottom. Your glance falls on the door of the storeroom – maybe that would be a good place to hide for a while and think up a plan. Quickly glancing up and down to make sure no one's coming, you scuttle inside.

Gain 1 ABILITY point and turn to **272**.

11

As you whip into a sharp turn, starting your descent towards the war engine, you see a long line of shining figures coming over a ridge ahead.

"*Interesting!*" whispers the Iron Smith.

The light is shining from the spear tips and polished armour of a band of ghostly riders. Iron Mane whips over the line as a ghost herald on a frisky pony raises a war-trumpet shaped like a boar's head to his lips. The trumpet brays a warning that turns the heads of the lizardfolk. Then the Knights of the Evening Star charge, bright banners fluttering as they silently surge down the hillside and break like a golden wave on the war engines. Their horses' hooves don't mark the turf, but their long lances strike true. The galloping ghosts drive forward, gouging deeper and deeper until the lizardfolk run for their lives, leaving their broken machines behind.

"*You have powerful friends,*" says the Iron Smith approvingly. "*I do believe the wizard is getting worried.*"

Turn to **274**.

12

You crouch and get ready as the metal monster bears down on you. At the last second, you jump up and toss the blanket over its head. It falls perfectly, just as you planned, wrapping around its helmet and tangling up its arms. But the suit of armour hardly seems to notice and doesn't stop. It swipes at you with a heavy iron fist, catching you on the side of the head. Cursing, you stumble away. You're going to need a new plan, and fast.

Deduct 1 LIFE point and delete the BLANKET from your LOG BOOK.

If you have a ROPE and want to try to trip up the armour, turn to **123**.

Otherwise, turn to **211**.

13

"Please, you must trust me," the old lady says, trying to calm the crowd. But no one believes her and the grumbling is spreading. Everyone is far too distracted to notice you, as you slip forward towards her barrel. You position yourself right below her as she waits for the crowd to settle, and from this distance you can see how anxious she looks. Before your nerves can get the better of you, you leap up, throw back your hood and hold the ring high in the air.

"Fear not! I've brought the Night Ring!" you shout.

Chaos breaks out immediately. Half the crowd start screaming, while the other half pull out their weapons and point them at you. In the midst of all the shouting, a rotten turnip sails out of the crowd and smashes into the side of your head. It is, without doubt, a very dramatic entrance.

The old lady seems less surprised than the others. She nods at you and smiles.

"I knew you would come," she whispers. "I saw you in my dreams." Then she raises her voice, shouting over the confusion. "Did I not say this would happen? Did I not foresee it? The ringbearer is here!"

"But it's a filthy goblin!" someone shouts.

She stares sternly in the direction of the shout, takes your hand and raises it over her head. "This is our champion," she says. "And we don't have a second to spare."

Deduct 1 LIFE point and gain 1 ABILITY point, then turn to **242**.

14

You drag on the lever, but it's rusted into position and the cart won't turn.

"*Hang on!*" screams Boggo.

Before you can brace yourself, the cart smashes into the rubble and jumps in the air. You're thrown against the side of the cart, and the violence of the impact sends an item spinning out of your pack. With an almighty thump, the cart wheels somehow crash back down on the left-hand track, and you race off again into the darkness.

"This is the best fun EVER!" squeaks Boggo as you pick up speed.

Delete one item from your LOG BOOK and turn to **299**.

15

You bind some tubes together to make a rope. Whenever a plant twitches, you blow your whistle and it falls asleep again like a baby hearing a lullaby. In a few moments you lower yourself over the side of the balcony, glad to leave the strange garden behind you. You drop safely to the tiles below.

Turn to **302**.

16

The item you've chosen is well made, but not at all magical. You pass it from hand to hand, hoping to discover some kind of enchantment in it, but there's nothing there.

"Oh no!" hisses Boggo. *"You took too long! Someone's coming!"*

Turn to **333**.

17

You reach for your weapon – but before you can draw it a huge branching limb reaches out of the forest and smashes you to the ground. The tree dragon smoothly emerges from between the trees – it must have been standing there watching you all the time.

"I TOLD YOU. DO NOT HARM MY CREATURES. YOU ARE AS BAD AS THE OTHERS AND YOU MUST DIE."

It picks you up and throws you as hard and as far as it can. Briefly, you fly like a bird above the treetops, seeing the whole forest spread out beneath you like an emerald carpet... until your little flight comes to a spiky, deadly end.

18

You row on for several hours, until you arrive beneath the shattered arch of Rocklaw Bridge. You've never seen it before, but even in its ruined state it's huge and imposing and you struggle to imagine the ancient creatures who apparently built it. Staring into the water, you have a sudden yearning to just throw the ring into it and run as far away as possible from this whole adventure. But then the image of Boggo's lifeless body hitting the ground comes back to you and you jump ashore and push your boat out into the river. Hoping you've left no traces for anyone to follow, you watch the boat drift into the darkness before you scramble up the bank.

Turn to **353**.

19

Despite your best efforts, you can't find the source of the rot. The stench of death and the moaning of the ghosts eventually grows too much to bear, so you return to the dragon with a heavy heart.

"I'm sorry," you say, removing the ring. "I failed." The tree dragon seems oddly calm though.

"IT WAS NOT THE TIME FOR THE CURSE TO DIE," it bellows. "PERHAPS THERE WILL BE ANOTHER TIME. THANK YOU FOR TRYING. COME – I WILL LEAD YOU TO YOUR CAVES."

Turn to **50**.

20

They rush past and you hold your breath until the butler and the hobtoads are gone. Then you jump out of your hiding place and hurry in the opposite direction, spiralling down the endless steps. After a while you realise you're just by the storeroom, about halfway down the tower. You hear more feet stamping up the stairs towards you. Taking no risks this time, you scuttle into the silent storeroom to work out what to do next.

Turn to **272**.

21

You peer at the keyholes and examine the different keys, holding each one up to the glimmering light. Quickly you identify the two with the correct shapes and slot them into the holes. Taking a deep breath, you twist them both at the same time. They move smoothly in the locks and all of the gates in the wall slide open. Lava surges down the channels, lighting up the forge as it bubbles through. You hear ancient gears begin to hiss and hum, and the Smith sounds almost impressed:

"Many have failed here, goblin. You begin to show promise..."

Gain 1 ABILITY point and turn to **5**.

22

As you enter the graveyard, a misty shape rises out of the ground, and then another... ghosts! Soon they're emerging from every grave, nodding to you and waving greetings. So Boggo was right – because you're carrying the ring, you can see them. One of them reaches out to you and tries to grasp your sleeve, but their touch is feather-soft. The ghosts – who are almost all goblins – look pleased to see you.

"That's it! That's it!" says the voice. *"Over here, there's a good goblin!"*

Some of the ghosts are wearing rags and some are wearing beautiful old-fashioned outfits. Some carry tools or treasured things: you spot a blacksmith with his hammer and a child with a ragdoll toy. Finally you reach the one who's been talking to you. He's sitting on a big, fancy tomb, wearing an apron and round spectacles.

"Well met, ringbearer!" he cries. *"I've been watching you advance through the woods. You glow, my friend! A glow delightful as the morning sun! The name's Shuggy, by the by!"*

The other ghosts gather around you, watching.

"Why can you talk?" you ask. "All the others are silent."

"My companions are all happily dead – particularly as they have the honour of seeing the ringbearer," says Shuggy cheerfully. "But I made a terrible promise! And now I want you to set me free from it. I swear it will help you on your quest, ringbearer."

"Quest? Ringbearer?" you mutter. It's odd how these ghosts seem to know everything already. You check the woods behind you – but there's no sign of anyone chasing you yet.

"I'm in a bit of hurry," you say.

"It won't take long! I just need you to solve a riddle. I was an inventor of genius while I breathed (though I say so myself), and when I died, I swore I'd give my greatest invention to the first goblin clever enough to deserve it. Well, I've been waiting and waiting and no one's come along these seventy years and more. I'm BORED, sir!"

"OK I'll try," you say. "I've always liked riddles."

"Splendid!" cries Shuggy. "My riddle's simple. All you have to do is tell me how old I was when I died. The answer's on my gravestone. I can give you one clue. You'll have to use every letter once. Oh, and there's a little rhyme to help you too. Not the greatest verse in the world, but it might just help you...

> *If you first find a bee,*
> *Then spiral, anti-clockwise,*
> *You will set me free,*
> *And win a very special prize."*

Turn the page and look at the picture of Shuggy's grave.
If you can work out how old he was when he died, turn to that number.

If you can't work it out, turn to **234**.

BORIS
AND
GWEN
DOBBER,
HAPPY
TOGETHER
FOREVER

BOBO
THE
JESTER
HE
LAUGHED
LAST

VALDA
WIZZING
WE WILL
REMEMBER HER
PUDDINGS
458-67

TERRYJON
ALSO KNOWN AS
"WINKER"
REST IN
GLORY.

23

You roll as you land, cracking the tiles but preserving your bones. A master assassin couldn't have done it better. With a new spring in your step, you continue your escape.

Gain 1 ABILITY point and turn to **302**.

24

You move your finger over the map, trying to remember how Darkmoon described Crow Cave, and then you spot it – a ruined fortress with a waterfall beneath it. That must be it. You tap the cave with your finger and feel something underneath. Lifting up the map, you see a folded parchment. The heading at the top reads: "Top Secret – Crow Cave." As you skim through the text, one phrase jumps out at you: "*Rumours of a secret entrance hidden behind the waterfall.*" You scrunch up the parchment and throw it into the fire.

Write down SECRET ENTRANCE in your LOG BOOK. If you find the waterfall at the entrance to Crow Cave, turn back 30 entries from the number you're on to try and find the secret entrance.

You're conscious that there's no time to lose, but the impressive array of weapons displayed on the wall catches your eye.

"*Might be an idea to climb out here,*" says Boggo, pointing to the vines that frame the window. "*Safer than the stairs.*"

If you want to take the time to steal a weapon, turn to **295**.

To climb out of the window on the vines, turn to **168**.

If you want to use the staircase to escape, turn to **62**.

25

Your apology works. The creature doesn't strike again, but it takes all your courage to stand there without running away.

"MY LAW IS SIMPLE," it says. "DO NOT HARM MY CREATURES OR MY FOREST."

"Alright," you say. "Very good. I won't touch a thing."

"THAT WILL INCREASE YOUR CHANCES OF SURVIVAL," says the dragon. It twitches its tail, made of twisted vines and bark, then steps back into the forest and vanishes, leaving you standing, breathless and shaken, among the silent trees. When you start walking again, you're very aware that the dragon may be watching you. After a while, you stop by a stream and drink the clear spring water. Refreshed, you notice a patch of blueberries growing by the side of the water. Your stomach is growling with hunger – but you remember the dragon's warning. Would eating berries be *harming* the forest though?

To pick some berries and eat them, turn to **227**.

To move on with an empty stomach, turn to **42**.

26

There are two paths that take you deeper into the cave: a set of stairs leads down to your left, where something is still roaring in the darkness, while a minecart stands at the top of a steep track down to your right.

"*I think you should go this way,*" says Boggo. He's perched himself on the rim of the minecart, waggling his legs. "*Don't like the sound of that roaring – and a little cart ride is going to be so much faster!"*

If you want to take the staircase, turn to **60**.

If you want to ride the minecart, turn to **267**.

27

The orb wobbles up to you menacingly. It has no eyes or arms or teeth but somehow you know it wants to gobble you up. The bones lodged inside it are bright white and you can see the half-digested body of a rat stuck just beneath the surface.

If you have some MAGMA HOT SAUCE, turn to **205**.

If you don't, turn to **113**.

28

"What are you doing here?" Midge whispers. Her eyes are red and watering from the onion-cutting, but she keeps on chopping. You don't know how to explain what's happened. Midge grew up with you and has always been your friend, but this feels too big to just blurt out.

"Don't stand idle," she hisses. "You'll get us both a beating. Sweep up all that onion skin."

You do as you're told and the sharp smell of onions rises around you.

"He killed Boggo," you say. For a moment you see it all happening again, the black light, the thump as his body hit the ground.

"He? You mean the Master?"

You nod. "Snuffed him out, like it was nothing."

Midge shudders. "Poor Boggo. He never deserved that. None of us do."

"*Always liked Midge,*" says Boggo in your ear. "*She's a smart goblin.*"

"But why risk your neck to tell me?" says Midge. "You know you ain't allowed in here."

"I need a way out," you say.

"What's wrong with the usual door?"

You shrug. Midge squints at you, then looks worried.

"It's you that's caused the mayhem today? Are they looking for you? No, don't answer that. I don't want to know." She thinks for a moment. "Yes, there's another way out. Through the cellars there's a tunnel – it'll take you to the big fields over by Blackwell. There'll be guards on the door of course."

"*Hey, Blackwell! That's where my folks live!*" says Boggo. "*We can go visit.*"

"How many guards?" you ask, ignoring him.

"I dunno. Three or four?" She nods over her shoulder. "The stairs down to the cellar are in that corner. Carry that basket of bones down there so it don't look suspicious. Then follow the big cobbled corridor. You can't miss it."

"Thanks Midge," you say.

"Go!" she says. She looks you in the eyes for a long moment. "And take care of yourself."

You pick up the basket of bones and head to the cellar.

Turn to **187**.

You point at the wolf-faced general.

"It's her," you say.

"*Very good, ringbearer,*" says the Iron Smith with a little chuckle. "*Now whisper my name in her ear and tell her to wake up.*"

You step over to the statue, which is still standing perfectly still.

"The Iron Smith tells you to wake up," you whisper. Instantly, she springs to life and stands to attention.

"*What are your orders, commander?*" she says – even though her eyes and her mouth don't move. You have no idea what to say. Behind her, thousands of iron feet stamp as one, as the entire army salutes you, the noise echoing through the cavern like a mighty drum.

"*Well?*" asks the Iron Smith. "*What would you have them do, ringbearer? Perhaps you are finally beginning to understand the power you hold on your finger? You could build your own empire with these soldiers. Think of that! They will do everything you say.*" Despite the great danger you're in and the urgency of your quest, the thought of being so powerful sends a shiver of excitement through you.

"I want you to help my friends fight their battle," you eventually say to the wolf general. "It will be starting very soon up there." You point at the ceiling.

"*We will try our best, commander,*" says the statue. "*But our journey to the surface will not be simple or swift. Look for us as the sun sets. We will not shy from battle.*"

Make a note in your LOG BOOK about the SUNSET PROMISE. If you see the setting sun at any point in your adventure, turn back 20 entries from the number you're on.

The general turns without a word and marches off. With a rhythmic clanking, the entire army falls into line behind her and follows her out of the square, their metal feet stepping in perfect time. The steady beat shakes dust from the ceiling far above and sends shivers through the ground, as you and Boggo hurry off towards the bridge that leads to the forge.

Turn to **180**.

30

You scuttle and weave, moving fast and then slow, with all your finely tuned goblin sense for sneaking. All the time you're trying not to think about the eyes in the sky and the fact that only the fiercest and most determined goblins are chosen to be bat-riders. Boggo would never have been one. You arrive in the safety of the chimney stacks and try the door... unlocked! Inside you find a rickety ladder and you scramble down it. At the bottom is a dark cupboard filled with long-handled brushes and a jumble of ash-streaked buckets – a chimney sweep's equipment. On the other side of the cupboard door, you hear the mayhem of the kitchen. The fearsome head chef Groucho is bellowing...

"Don't put MUSHROOMS in a CELERY SOUP!"

Taking a moment to settle yourself, you ease the door open and slide into the kitchen.

Turn to **222**.

31

The guard-ghoul lands a series of vicious blows, pushing you further and further towards the window. Its next attack sends your weapon spinning across the floor, and as you try to dart forward to retrieve it the ghoul picks you up and hurls you out of the window with a savage cackle. Darkmoon's butler finds your body a few hours later, and leaves it on display to discourage any other rebellious goblins.

32

But how do you destroy the ring? Your confusion must show on your face, because Boggo grins.

"You've got the power, friend. You've always had it, right from the start. Just think it and you'll make it so."

"Just think?" you say. "Alright..."

The instant you decide to destroy the ring, it shatters into a fine black powder. The Iron Smith's voice falls silent and you feel his presence drifting off. All around you, the iron army are motionless, frozen in place again. Boggo's ghost is already fading away.

"Boggo! I'm... sorry," you say. As a tear rolls down your cheek, you realise that you hadn't properly mourned him in these last few mad days. That's because he was there all along, still joking and grumbling, still Boggo. But now you're really going to lose him.

"I couldn't have done it, Boggo. Not without you. You're the greatest friend," you splutter. He's fading so quickly that you can hardly hear what he's saying.

"Live... a good life... friend... I'll see you in... the next..."

Then a breath of evening breeze carries him away into the star-filled sky.

In the years that follow, your life is simple and happy, and nothing very exciting ever happens to you again. In fact, as time passes it's hard to believe that the whole adventure ever happened at all. One summer's evening, on the 46th anniversary of the Battle of Crow Cave (as it became known), you're sitting in your garden, half-asleep, watching your children and grandchildren splashing in the pond below. Your bench is beneath the branches of a big oak tree that you planted yourself when you first bought the farm. As the light fades and your eyelids droop, your thoughts turn to Boggo, whom you still miss every day. But you don't regret the choice you made on that battlefield so many years ago.

"*And you shouldn't, friend...*" says a voice beside you. You hear it quite clearly, as if he was sitting right there on the bench. You turn, and there he is, grinning his grin.

"*Boggo!*"

"*Time for another adventure, old friend.*"

He gets to his feet and points up at the sky. As you rise to follow, feeling more nimble than you have in years, you slip out of your body and leave it behind, sitting there on the bench.

"*I'm dead, aren't I?*" you ask, suddenly a little afraid. "*What happens now?*"

"*O-ho!*" Boggo chuckles. "*Just wait and see...*"

33

"You were thirty-three years old," you say. "A good age for a goblin."

"*Well done, sir!*" cries the ghost. "*I knew you could do it. You don't know what it's been like, waiting here in the graveyard for a goblin with a first-rate mind to wander along. Who'd have thought it would take seventy years?*"

You check behind you again. Still no one chasing you, but you know every second could be vital.

"*Ah excuse me, ringbearer,*" chortles Shuggy. "*You're in a hurry and here I am blathering on. Let me get your reward. My greatest invention: Shuggy's Shatterproof Shield!*"

You hear a grinding noise and then a door hinges open at the base of the statue. Inside is a thick, bronze-coloured bracelet.

"*Take it!*" cries Shuggy. "*It's a very nifty device. Completely collapsible, wrist-carried, portable protection! You just press that little button there.*"

You slip the bracelet on your wrist and press the button. A shield flips out, unfolding to an impressive size.

"*It's very light because it's made with barillium,*" says Shuggy. "*You'll find it highly useful...*"

Add the SHATTERPROOF SHIELD in your LOG BOOK. Make a note that it will stop the first successful attack by an enemy in any battle you fight. After that, continue the fight as normal.

"Thank you Shuggy," you say. "But now I have to go."

"*I understand!*" says Shuggy. "*Go! Defeat Darkmoon! We're all behind you!*"

As you're leaving the graveyard, you look back and see that he's grown faint and blurry like the other ghosts. They're all waving.

Turn to **101**.

34

You find yourself on a windswept, treeless ledge with a sheer drop all along one side. There's one more hill ahead before you reach the top. Halfway up the hill in the distance you can see a new track that turns down towards a wooded valley, and there's an ancient waystone where the two tracks meet. Perhaps there are some directions to Crow Cave scratched into the stone? As you set off to find out, a terrible shriek comes from the sky. A moment later a bat-rider dives towards you out of the low cloud, its lance pointing at your throat. There's no time to hide. You keep your eyes on the tip of the lance and roll out of the way at the last second. The deadly point scrapes across your back and you hear the rider's grunt of irritation as it soars away to mount another attack. It dives once more and again you manage to dodge away, but you now find yourself right on the edge of the cliff.

You can't run, and you can't keep dodging. And if you try to attack the bat, the rider will kill you with his lance before you're near enough to land a blow. You decide that your only hope is to throw a weapon at the bat and try to surprise it. Keeping your eyes on the sinister wings as it swoops down again for the killing blow, you take aim and get ready to throw.

Choose the WEAPON you want to throw from your LOG BOOK, then roll one dice and add your STRENGTH and WITS levels.

If your total is 9 or higher, turn to **175**.

If your total is 8 or lower, turn to **83**.

35

You draw your weapon and swing wildly at the armour but the rusting metal keeps stomping forward as you dance just out of its reach. It's hard to be nimble on the swampy ground and when you stumble a metal fist crunches into the side of your head. You try to strike back, jabbing at its knee joint, but your attack bounces off and doesn't slow the armour down at all. You aren't going to be able to beat this thing in a fight. Starting to panic, you scramble out of the trench and run.

Deduct 2 LIFE points and turn to **169**.

36

You're far too good at tumbling to be snapped up by a plant. You scamper away to safety as the giant flower returns to its meal. Now you need a way off this balcony.

Turn to **4**.

37

You've never been this close to one of the giant minotaurs. Even sitting down it's huge – muscles coil in its back like snakes as it turns towards you.

"Hello there, little one," it rumbles, and then stiffens, as it sniffs at you. Its eyes go wide. "Do not be afraid. I will not give away your secret."

It knows? You're too shocked to reply.

"There is not much time, so listen. You must be careful, little one," says the minotaur. "Your enemies will sniff out that powerful thing you carry, just as I did. Allow me to help you. Take this charm. Hang it around your neck. It will mask the scent of magic on your skin."

"Why are you helping me?" you ask.

"Because if Darkmoon is defeated my people will be freed from our suffering. We all wish you well, little one. We have been waiting for you for a long time."

"What – *waiting for me?*" you say.

"There is no time to explain. You must escape. Take our gift and go."

If you want to hang the MINOTAUR'S CHARM around your neck, write it down in in your LOG BOOK. Whenever you roll a dice for your RING TRACKER during your adventure, add 2 to the roll.

"But..." you say.

"Go," says the minotaur. "We've already talked for too long..."

If you want to look for another way out, turn to **327**.

If you want to talk to the lizardfolk, turn to **275**.

38

You quickly climb the scaffolding to investigate the problem. The iron is slippery, but there are plenty of holds and you are soon crouched above the place where the water is splashing out of control. You can see that fallen rocks have blocked a pipe, and the water is surging around it. A few deft kicks, and the blockage clears. The water flows true now, funnelling down the chutes into the tangle of pipes at the bottom that draw the water out into the forge.

"*Good goblin! Now you are ready to light the forge!*" booms the Iron Smith.

Gain 1 ABILITY point and turn to **153**.

39

As you continue through the empty city towards the forge, you catch glimpses of what life was once like here: a market scattered with broken glass, a park filled with trees that have turned to stone, a huge pile of rubble in the middle of the street. There's a lot to look at, which is why you don't pay too much attention to the debris until you're walking past it. You only realise your mistake when you see steam hissing from a pair of huge green nostrils sticking out from beneath the bricks. A low rumbling noise shivers your bones.

"*Erm, is that snoring coming from a... dragon?*" squeaks Boggo.

You gasp, and freeze as you realise a sleeping dragon is only a few yards away. You can feel the heat radiating off its scales, even though its body is covered in dust and bricks.

As you stand there, wondering what to do, the dragon hums in her sleep. The sound is so low it's hard to make out, but the tune feels sad.

If you have a MYSTERIOUS EGG, turn to **207**.

If you don't...

To try to sneak past the dragon, turn to **142**.

To try to wake the dragon up and talk to it, turn to **286**.

To attack the dragon before it can attack you, turn to **355**.

40

There isn't much cover on the stairs, but the shutters on a window offer a little nook to hide in. You fold yourself into the shadows, close your eyes, hold your breath and pray. Dozens of boots are thundering towards you. You know that if they spot you, you're doomed.

Roll one dice and add it to your SNEAK level.

If your total is 4 or higher, turn to **20**.

If your total is 3 or lower, turn to **350**.

41

"ATTACK!"

A deafening metallic shout rings out across the battlefield, loud enough to drag your attention away from the sunset and your imminent death. The noise is so loud that even Darkmoon turns to look, suddenly a little uncertain. And that tiny hesitation is the only opportunity that Iron Mane needs – diving down out of nowhere, it swoops in and carries you up and away from the wreckage of the castle, the pale fire fading away as you gain height.

Then you see what made the noise. The iron army, glinting in the last rays of the dying sun, has kept its promise to you. Marching forwards, they attack Darkmoon's soldiers with mechanical precision as swords and axes and arrows bounce harmlessly off their metal bodies. Now the enemy troops are running for their lives, leaving the corpses of their fallen comrades behind. With a scream of rage, Darkmoon stares up at you and launches a burst of raw magic at Iron Mane. The horse dips and the flames fizz just over your heads.

"*Now we fight together, goblin,*" says the Iron Smith calmly. "*We may lose perhaps, but not for want of courage. It has been an honour to fight with you.*" And with that the great metal beast folds its wings and drops down on Darkmoon like a thunderbolt, as he mutters the incantation to summon another spell. You and Iron Mane must fight the wizard to the death.

DARKMOON

Rounds: 8   Damage: 1

YOU

If you win, turn to **279**.

If you lose, turn to **202**.

42

Gradually the forest changes. The trees to the left of the path are just the same, growing thick and straight and green – but to the right, the wood is covered in a strange, foul-smelling black rot. Many trees have died, choked by the black stuff, and you keep as far away from it as you can. As you trudge along, trying to ignore the stench, you find yourself wondering what's happened to Boggo – you haven't seen him since you came into the forest hours ago. You're just wondering what kind of joke he would make about the rot when you hear a terrifying howl from that side of the forest. Suddenly a big dark shape comes crashing towards you, smashing the trees aside as it rampages towards the road. Your hand goes to your weapon, but you remember the tree dragon's warning: "DO NOT HARM MY CREATURES OR MY FOREST..."

If you want to run away, turn to **100**.

If you want to stand your ground and fight, turn to **291**.

43

You feel a lot safer once you're under the shelter of the branches, although you notice the tree trunks are blackened as though they were recently burned. After walking a little way you come across an abandoned cabin. Its windows are boarded up and the door hangs loosely on its hinges.

To sneak around the cabin and carry on to Blackwell, turn to **82**.

To have a look inside the cabin, turn to **105**.

44

As you try to sneak past the snail, your foot taps against a rock. It only makes the faintest noise – but that's all the snail needs. Abandoning its meal, it lunges towards you with a sickening slurp. Grasping tentacles snatch at your limbs as it tries to drag you into its razor-toothed mouth.

VAMPIRE SNAIL

Rounds: 3 Damage: 2

YOU

If you win, turn to **140**.

If you lose, turn to **326**.

45

Cupping your hands, you lift the green liquid to your lips and drink deeply. The taste is wonderfully refreshing and a golden warmth spreads through your body, right to the tips of your toes.

Gain 1 ABILITY point and add 3 LIFE points.

Your eyes are closed, so you don't notice the metal plate slide over the basin, hiding the egg away. By the time you look down again, there's no way to get it. You carefully retrace your steps back to the entrance and head down the stairs.

Turn to **120**.

46

The compass needle swings so wildly about that you wonder if there's too much old magic in the marsh for it to work. Finally, it settles on one direction and sticks to it. If the compass is right, you need to take the left-hand path to Crow Cave.

To trust the compass and take the left-hand path, turn to **51**.

To choose the other path, turn to **300**.

47

With the wind howling and your body flipping this way and that, you pull yourself back towards the saddle. Iron Mane swerves wildly, trying to stay ahead of the green fire, but the magic missile is too fast.

"*LET GO YOU FOOL!*" screams the Smith. But it's too late. Darkmoon's flaming dart explodes as it catches you and blasts you into unconsciousness. You fall from the saddle and drop a very long way. The ground finishes the job.

48

Gradually, the trees around the path begin to change. More and more of them are covered in patches of a strange black rot that is part mushroom and part slime and stinks like dying things. You're careful not to touch it. Many of the infected trees have fallen, and no new ones grow in their place. The dragon doesn't seem to be following you now and you wonder if it's afraid of the rot. You're afraid too, but you're committed now, so, for a long time, you walk on through the dying wood – until you find your path completely blocked by a giant, fallen oak covered in lumpy, mushroomy growths. There's no safe way around it: you're going to have to climb over it, trying not to come into contact with the black stuff.

Roll one dice and add it to your SNEAK level.

If your total is 6 or higher, turn to **150**.

If your total is 5 or lower, turn to **7**.

49

You land on the roof with a tile-shattering thump, and something pops in your ankle as you crunch down. Wincing and rubbing your leg, you glance about the rooftops.

Deduct 1 LIFE point and turn to **302**.

You're at the edge of the forest now, and the tree dragon leads you out into the open, away from the cover of the trees. Thick mist hangs in the valley beyond, but you can see a chalky white path winding up through the dark thickets of bracken.

"GOOD LUCK, GOBLIN," says the dragon, then turns and melts back into the forest. Once the trees have stopped rustling, you would never know it had been there.

Turn to **250**.

51

As you walk further into the marsh you begin to see the ruins of huge rusting cannons and catapults, half-sunk in the swamp – there was definitely a big battle here once. There's a strange buzzing in the air, as if millions of flies were swarming in the distance. You're no sorcerer, but it feels as though terrible magic was done in this place.

The mist is thinning now so you keep an eye on the skies but there's no sign of the bat-riders yet. You pick your way past deep craters filled with oily water, and shattered boulders. Rusted weapons stick out of the muck like strange plants, and in the distance you can see dozens of ragged banners planted in the ground. You're approaching the first banner – which flutters twenty feet up in the air – when a voice calls out to you.

"*Hey! Goblin! Are you a sight for sore eyes!*" It chuckles. "*If I had eyes, that is.*"

The voice is alarmingly loud after the silence of your long walk – but you can't see anyone.

"Where are you?" you say.

"*Down here, chum. In the puddle. A poor cursed soul, trapped by magic.*"

You peer into the water by the side of the path. A face is looking up at you – a goblin's face, shadowy and vague.

"You're a ghost?" you say.

"*Indeed I am,*" it replies. "*The name's Stinker.*"

Stinker pulls off his head, as if he was lifting his cap to you in greeting. "*I was wondering if you could do me a favour. See, I've lost my skull and until I get it back, I can't leave this place.*"

You look about. The ground here beneath the banners looks dangerous, full of deep puddles with unknown dangers lurking in them. You shake your head doubtfully.

"*Look! I'll make it worth your while,*" says Stinker. "*I know where a magic sword is buried, see? Get me my skull, and I'll show you the spot.*"

You try to make out his expression, but the features are slippery and blurred.

If you want to help the goblin ghost find his skull, turn to **125**.

If you want to move on, turn to **201**.

52

You've only taken two steps into the room when a cloud of green gas squirts up from the floor. Choking, you stumble back to the staircase, your throat burning as if the air itself is on fire.

Deduct 3 LIFE points and turn to **120**.

53

The map on the table is covered in notes and papers. Little counters show how the Master's search for the rebels is going. There's a lot of information to take in. You try to remember what Crow Cave looked like in the mirror. Can you find it on the map?

Look at the picture on the next page. If you can work out where Crow Cave is, use its grid reference on the left to find the first number, and its grid reference at the top to find the second number. Multiply the two numbers together and turn to that entry.

If you can't work it out, turn to **106**.

54

The orb turns with surprising speed and tries to block your escape, but you just manage to stay ahead of it.

Roll one dice and add it to your STRENGTH level.

If your total is 5 or higher, turn to **258**.

If your total is 4 or lower, turn to **27**.

55

You haven't even taken a step before a new voice calls out to you.

"*Ringbearer. Look up.*" The voice is deep, old and commanding – as though it's used to being obeyed. You do as you're told, and see that the banner above your head isn't faded anymore. Instead it glows rich purple with bright gold thread and it's fluttering in a ghostly breeze that doesn't bend the marsh reeds or ripple the water. Stitched onto the banner is a picture of a knight in armour, and he's looking down at you.

"*You did a kind thing for that goblin, ringbearer,*" he says. "*And you were not rewarded. This I find unjust, so I would like to give you something of mine.*"

"Who are you?" you ask gruffly, suspicious of more ghostly tricks.

"*It matters not who I am,*" says the stitched knight. "*Only that I died on this very spot, fighting to overthrow the vicious tyrant who owned that ring you have in your pocket. I took you at first for a common goblin thief, but I start to see that your purpose may be more noble than that. If you are that wizard's enemy, then you are a friend of mine. You will find my blade by the base of this banner. Take it with my blessing, and may it bring you better luck than it brought me.*"

You reach down into the muck and pull out a gleaming silver

weapon. It's not much larger than a dagger, and it shines as if it was forged today.

"*Now go,*" says the knight. "*And know that when the time comes, the Knights of the Evening Star will stand with you.*"

The banner droops and its colours fade again. Just at that moment, the mist shifts and you catch a glimpse of a hill in the distance with a ruined castle crouched at the top. Crow Cave...

Add the LUCK BLADE to your LOG BOOK. If you fight with it, once in every combat you can reroll the lowest dice of an attack roll and pick the best result.

Gain 1 ABILITY point and turn to **250**.

56

As you approach the dock, you only notice the tall figure leaning against a post at the last moment. It's wearing black robes and its face is wreathed in shadows – a guard-ghoul, one of the Master's most dangerous soldiers. It's watching you closely. You try your best to look innocent, but it does no good: the ghoul steps out in front of you to block your path.

"*Now what would a goblin in the uniform of a tower servant be doing out here?*" it rasps.

"I'm off duty," you say, trying to keep your voice casual. It tilts its head slowly and looks at you, like a cat deciding whether to pounce on a mouse.

"*You're coming with me, goblin,*" it says suddenly, grabbing your arm with its iron-gloved fingers. You're in big trouble now and you immediately think of the ring. It could probably save your life, but it's a big risk – the last time you used it Darkmoon noticed. So maybe you could beat this thing in a normal fight? Whatever you decide, you need to decide right now...

To attack the guard-ghoul, turn to **253**.

To use the ring, turn to **166**.

57

You snatch up the stool as an improvised weapon and smash it on her head. You've made her dizzy now, so you might just stand a chance.

HOBTOAD GUARD

Rounds: 4 Damage: 1

YOU

If you knock the hobtoad out, turn to **225**.

If you lose, turn to **92**.

58

You defend yourself ferociously, slashing away at the orb every time it come close. It bumps and lunges, feinting this way and that, but you hold firm and drive it off. Suddenly, it bobs away from you and squeezes back into the same doorway it came out of. Before it has a chance to change its mind, you dash out of the square.

Turn to **352**.

59

You climb away from the hornets as fast as you can.

Roll one dice and add it to your SNEAK level.

If your total is 6 or higher, turn to **265**.

If the total is 5 or lower, turn to **158**.

60

You tread carefully down the dark stairwell. Boggo disappears up ahead, and a few moments later comes back wide-eyed.

"You know that roaring sound? It's an absolutely massive snail! It glows, it's got tentacles and I wouldn't like to get too close to its teeth..."

You creep forward to have a look. Boggo's not lying about the size of the snail, the tentacles or its teeth. It's sitting in the middle of the corridor chewing on a bone.

If you have a BAT WHISTLE or a WOODEN WHISTLE,

turn to **75**.

To try sneaking quickly past the snail, turn to **130**.

If you want to go back and try the minecart instead, turn to **267**.

61

Darkmoon strides towards you, breaking into a smile as he sees your terrified face.

"Did you really think it would be that easy, goblin?" he sneers, as flames still lick across his robes. "Really, I should thank you for making it so simple for me. You've brought my property right back to me – most kind of you. For that, I will make your death quick. Then I will take back my ring – and crush the rebels once and for all."

He raises his hand and pale fire crackles from his fingertips and lifts you into the air. You try to use the ring, but your lips are frozen and your fingers won't move. Darkmoon is walking slowly forwards and you look away from his dreadful smile, up into the sky.

"Your little horse won't save you this time, goblin," says the wizard. "It would seem that you've run out of friends."

But you aren't looking for Iron Mane. Your eyes are fixed on the western hills and the setting sun, which is burning the sky crimson and gold. Not a bad thing to look at as you die.

"*You did your best,*" whispers Boggo. "*Thank you, my friend.*"

And then the pale fire crackles around you, and it's done.

62

You trot down the stairs trying to look innocent and calm. You're just another servant lost in the confusion. Boggo has vanished, but his warning was right – a line of hobtoad guards is blocking the staircase.

"In there goblin," orders one of them, pointing to the door. "One of youse is in BIG trouble."

There's no way you can break through and escape – and you don't think you can talk your way past them either. Silently cursing your choice, you shuffle towards the door. The guards push you down a corridor and into a room at the rear of the tower on the back stairs.

Turn to **173**.

63

You saunter confidently among the tents, doing your best to blend in with the crowd and trying to move like a human. The cave is humming with activity: solders are bustling about carrying weapons and supplies while kids chase each other and their parents whisper in worried clusters. The smell of freshly baked bread adds a homely touch to the tense atmosphere.

Boggo's ghost flickers to life beside you.

"*Look sharp*," he cackles. "*This place is busier than a beehive at breakfast!*" You glance into a couple of tents looking for something useful. Inside one, a young healer is stitching a gash in a soldier's arm with skilful fingers, and inside the next you see piles of second-hand uniforms and clothes, presumably for new recruits to wear. Up ahead there's a bigger tent, made of crimson silk and guarded by two stern-looking humans. You don't think it would be a good idea to go there.

To look for a disguise in the uniform tent, turn to **190**.

To hang around and try to listen to what people are saying, turn to **99**.

64

The griefers' shrieks fade as you turn a corner and approach the forge's main entrance. It's a dramatic sight: half-temple and half-machine, with a huge iron staircase leading up into it. The forge is covered in gears and pistons, but none of them are moving. At the bottom of the staircase there's a mound of skulls, and as you approach a misty figure rises up from among the gleaming bones.

"*Stop there, ringbearer!*" It's a minotaur's ghost, twice your height, dressed in ancient armour that looks like a monk's robes and carrying a scythe. Her voice is old-fashioned and oddly musical.

"*You are not the first ringbearer I have faced here,*" she says, staring at you intently as though trying to peer into your mind. "*Though you are my first goblin...*"

"Why are you here?" you ask.

"*I am here because I must be here until the cycle is broken and that cursed ring is destroyed. That was my quest all those years ago – the quest that I failed, on these very steps.*"

"And... how long ago was that?"

"*Three thousand, two hundred and ninety-three years ago. And the ring was old even then.*" The minotaur sighs, and her shoulders droop as if the weight of all that time is a heavy burden. "*And when you fail – as I fear you will, goblin – you will be bound just as I am, by the ring's terrible curse.*"

"I'm not going to fail," you say. "I'm going to restart the forge and wake up the Smith. And I'm in a hurry, so if you don't mind..."

The minotaur raises her scythe and blocks your path as you try to step past her up the staircase. "*No, goblin. It is not only about waking the Smith, it is what comes next, once you hold everything you could ever wish for in the palm of your hand. Eternal power...*" Her eyes glitter darkly. "*Time after time, the ringbearer has failed in that final choice. Even I, Smyra Goldenheart, was not strong enough when that choice came. So what chance for a little goblin like you?*"

She looks deeply into your eyes.

If you have the MINOTAUR'S CHARM, turn to **229**.

If you don't:

If your RING SCORE is 3 or higher, turn to **340**.

If your RING SCORE is 2 or lower, turn to **247**.

65

Holding your breath, you step over the last strand of web. You're clear! Even better, you spot a large beetle trundling across the floor. Snatching up the crunchy snack before it can scuttle away, you gobble it down – it tastes just the right kind of salty. Feeling more cheerful, you hurry on.

Add 2 LIFE points and turn to **285**.

66

As you turn to run, you hear the cat's claws scratching across the floor behind you. Hissing, it leaps for your back.

Roll one dice and add your SNEAK level and your STRENGTH level.

If the total is 7 or higher, turn to **263**.

If the total is 6 or lower, turn to **179**.

67

You spot it at last: a black stone tangled in the roots of a mighty tree. Following the dragon's orders you touch the ring to the stone and it crumbles away like sand. A great sigh goes up: all across the forest, the rot is vanishing. The mushrooms dwindle, the stinking slime shrinks, and the ghosts fade away. They sigh softly as they are released. It takes just a few moments – and soon, although the damage remains, it's clear the curse has lifted.

"YOU ARE TRULY A FRIEND OF THE FOREST," booms the tree dragon. "WE WILL BE FOREVER IN YOUR DEBT."

"Thank you," you say. "But what I really need now is to get to Crow Cave before sundown."

"I WILL SHOW YOU THE WAY," says the dragon. "FIRST, PLEASE TAKE THIS ACORN AS A SYMBOL OF OUR FRIENDSHIP. IF YOU NEED US, WE WILL COME."

It reaches out a leafy limb, and you spot a golden acorn on one of the twigs. When you pick the acorn, you feel new strength running through your body.

"NOW FOLLOW ME," says the dragon.

Add 2 LIFE points and add the GOLDEN ACORN to your LOG BOOK, then turn to **50**.

68

You rush down the stairs, taking them two at a time. Behind you, the alarm wails. From below, you hear raised voices and urgent boots stamping up towards you. Your heart almost stops when you see the long crimson robes and frowning face of General Starr, the Master's most feared commander. He's accompanied by guard-ghouls – the deadliest soldiers in the tower. As the soldiers storm past you, the General halts.

"What did you see up there, goblin?" he growls. His skin is pale and rotten.

"S-sir..." you fumble for an answer. You've never spoken to him before.

"Out with it, halfwit!" he roars. "What set off the alarms?"

To say you saw a man in black upstairs, turn to **161**.

To say you saw nothing, turn to **318**.

69

You step deftly to the side as the wood creature passes, and then when it skids to a stop you raise your arms wide and make cooing noises. It's pure instinct: you used the same sounds to calm worried goats back on your parents' farm. To your surprise, it seems to work and it limps nervously towards you. Its body is woven from young, green shoots.

"There, there," you mutter, reaching out to pat it. It bows its head and you stroke the bark. "What's wrong with you?"

The sapling whines and tosses its head. You examine the foot that it was limping on and see something strange – buried in its hoof is a black, mushroomy growth. You find a stick by the side of the road and prise the growth loose. Eventually it comes away, and almost at once new bark grows over the wound. The sapling seems delighted and capers about the road making a high-pitched chuckling sound. When you walk on, it follows – it seems you have gained a companion.

Gain 1 ABILITY point and turn to **209**.

70

Just as you grab the whistle, you feel the plant's jaws close around your leg. Its needle-thin teeth stab through your skin, spreading a cold numbness into your body. Unable to kick yourself free, you raise the whistle to your lips and blow.

"This had better work," you think.

The note the whistle produces is low and pure. At once, all the plants' heads droop down as if they're asleep, and the giant fangs release your leg. Struggling to your feet, you limp away.

Deduct 1 LIFE point and 1 STRENGTH point. Add the WOODEN WHISTLE to your LOG BOOK.

Turn to **4**.

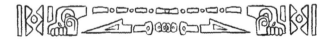

71

You take one of the great staircases down to the ruined city. Each identical step – and there are hundreds – has been carved out of the rock with perfect precision. As you get closer to the lava rivers, you start to sweat. The ground feels baking hot through the soles of your boots, and you wonder how the people who lived here managed to keep cool. You find yourself in a tangle of fallen buildings and drifting smoke. Relying on the map you made in your mind, you weave your way through the spookily empty streets.

Soon you reach an open square that you recognise because of the statue that still towers in the middle. It shows a shirtless giant with a chunky beard and a massive hammer raised high, ready to strike. As you hurry across the square, you notice movement in a doorway. A strange, floaty shape is squeezing out and heading straight for you. It looks like a huge ball of jelly, and several skeletons are stuck inside it, as well as ordinary household items like pans, chamber pots and hammers. As it squelches towards you with alarming speed, you have a couple of seconds to decide what to do.

To fight the jelly orb, turn to **27**.

To try and run away, turn to **54**.

72

You jump away from the door just in time. Rotten planks fly everywhere as the hog smashes it aside. She charges, trying to gore you with her tusks, but you land a sharp jab on her snout as she passes, and she squeals with surprise and dashes away. It all happens so fast that you can't quite believe you've managed to survive. There's nothing of value inside the abandoned cabin, so you head warily back out into the forest.

Gain 1 ABILITY point and turn to **82**.

73

You sift through the different keys, holding them up to the light and trying to match them to the shape of the keyholes. In the end you choose two that seem to be right and push them in. When you turn them, nothing happens so you turn a little harder. With a deafening bang, the mechanism explodes and blasts you to smithereens.

74

You don't feel like you have any choice but to give the girl something. Cross out ONE item from your LOG BOOK as you hand it to her.

"Thanks," she smiles. "I'll keep my mouth shut now. And here's a free bit of advice. You probably guessed the village is completely surrounded. The only way you're getting out of here alive is down the river, so I'd head to the jetty if I was you."

She jumps off the wall and disappears. You aren't sure you can trust her, but you don't have a better plan so you hurry off towards the river, clinging to the shadows.

Turn to **195**.

75

"D'you have anything that makes a noise?" asks Boggo.

You fish through your pockets and pull out the whistle.

"See, I think that snail's blind," he continues, *"so if you make a big noise here, and then quick and quiet scuttle over there, you'll be able to get past it no problem."*

Easy for you to say, you think to yourself. But you don't have a better plan so you do exactly as he suggests: your toot on the whistle draws the snail's attention and as it slithers eagerly towards the sound, you slip to the other side of the corridor. The noise of your footsteps is enough to alert the snail and it lurches towards you, but you've gained just enough space to jump over its tentacles as they flail for your dashing feet. Trying to ignore the terrible stink of the creature, you scramble away and flee.

"Knew we should have taken that minecart," mutters Boggo.

You run as fast as you can into a maze of corridors and staircases, and before you know it you're completely lost.

Turn to **356**.

76

"Goblins are all liars. I'm taking you in," snaps the hobtoad as she grabs for your neck and tries to collar you. You skip away and raise your fists. You've never been much good in a fight, but you're going to have to learn fast now. As you're fighting without a weapon, remember to subtract one from all your rolls.

HOBTOAD GUARD

Rounds: 4   Damage: 1

YOU

If you win, turn to **225**.

If you lose, turn to **92**.

77

You dodge this way and that, keeping the spider at bay and hacking at it when you get the chance. As you slice through more and more cobwebs, the spider gets increasingly agitated by the damage you're doing to its home. Eventually it's had enough and scuttles back up to the ceiling. From a safe distance, it waves its legs at you angrily. Without pausing to wave back, you run down the steps.

Turn to **285**.

78

Once you reach the huge slab of the door, the ring shivers in your pocket. You know what it wants you to do. But before you put it on, you turn and look back over your shoulder. "Good luck ringbearer," says the lady, and an answering murmur swells through the crowd.

"I'm going to need it," you think, and slip on the ring. The great slab begins to grind upwards, and as it slowly moves a new voice echoes in your mind. It's low and soft and gently amused, and somehow you know it's the Iron Smith talking. "*Enter, goblin. As is your destiny.*"

As soon as you step through the doorway, the slab slams down and you know there's no turning back. After the madness of the crowd, it's almost a relief. You're alone, in a dark corridor framed by huge stone blocks, and dimly lit by patches of glowmoss. The air smells dank and heavy, as if it hasn't been stirred in a thousand years.

Check your RING SCORE.

If it's 3 or more, turn to **259**.

If it's 2 or less, turn to **133**.

79

"This will help you light the fire," you say, pulling it from your bag and holding it out. "I know how hard it is to get warm in the rain." The father squints at you, still wary, and doesn't take it.

"I've never seen a goblin offer a kindness," he snaps. "Why should we trust you?"

"The old customs of the road say that I should help," you answer. "We follow them, just as you do."

The man furrows his brow, then nods and lowers his weapon. "Well, I can't say help would be unwelcome. These blasted logs are soaked through, and we've no dry tinder."

Working together, you get the fire lit. You don't worry about the bat-riders so much, since a human family is the last thing they'll be looking for. The children stare at you with a wide-eyed mixture of fear and fascination. They've probably never seen a goblin up close before, except in scary pictures of the villains in their story books. You pull a funny face at them and tell one of Boggo's jokes, and they relax a little. With the fire lit, a brew is soon bubbling in the kettle, and the parents explain that they left their home this morning to head for the hills because there's talk of a big battle in the next few days.

"No one wants to have one of Darkmoon's armies on their doorstep," explains the mum. "All those awful lizards and minotaurs and goblins... oh dear, I'm sorry, no offence intended."

You chuckle and take a sip of nettle tea, which warms you all the way down to your toes. Then you ask if they know the way to Crow Cave. Suddenly they look a little wary again. You do your best to reassure them that you aren't a spy, but there's an awkward silence until one of the kids blurts out: "Take the first turning on the right, by the aspen tree. Then look for the waterfall – that's where the entrance is. What, Mum? The goblin helped us. It's the custom of the road, a kindness for a kindness..."

The mother breaks into a smile, proud of her child and just about convinced that you're on the side of good. Swigging the last of your tea and shaking hands with each of them, you go on your way.

Add 1 LIFE point and turn to **341**.

80

Try as you might, the brake won't budge. The cart smashes straight through the rotten wood of the fence and over the lip of the drop. The fall lasts just long enough for you to wonder whether you're going to hit solid ground or lava. The fiery splosh you hear just before you die gives you the answer.

81

The liquid tastes surprisingly good – like honey and spices, with a fiery kick.

Add 3 LIFE points and turn to **4**.

82

You sneak on through the woods, occasionally checking over your shoulder to see if you're being followed. But everything is silent. Away to your right, the path to Blackwell cuts through the trees, but you don't dare move into the open. Even though the brambles are getting thicker, it feels much safer to stay under cover.

Roll one dice and add it to your WITS level.

If your total is 6 or higher, turn to **197**.

If your total is 5 or lower, turn to **290**.

83

You misjudge your throw and the weapon sails agonizingly wide. This time the rider ignores the lance and rides straight into you. The bat hammers you to the ground and pins you with its claws, its hot, stinking breath all around you as it leans in towards your throat. Desperate, you reach for the ring, scrunch your eyes shut and scream, "GET OFF ME!"

Immediately, the pressure lifts off your chest, and by the time your eyes are open the bat and its rider are tiny dots high in the sky, zooming straight up as though lifted by an invisible rope. You wrench the ring off your finger and watch them disappear before scrambling to your feet.

Fill in the next section of the RING TRACKER on your LOG BOOK, then roll one dice.

If the number is equal to or lower than your RING SCORE, turn to **297**.

If the total is higher than your RING SCORE, turn to **257**.

84

The red glow comes from lava seeping through cracks in the wall, and as you stare you realise there are several gates that are currently holding the lava back. You can hear the rumble and hiss of the molten rock behind the gates, and on the ground there are deep channels for it to flow into. In front of you is an iron pedestal with two large keyholes cut into it, and lots of different keys scattered around on top of it.

"*To fire my forge, you must open the gates in that wall, so the lava can bring my kingdom to life again,*" booms the Smith. "*But be careful, ringbearer – if you insert the wrong keys, the forge can be a little unforgiving. You have one chance only.*"

Look at the picture on the next page. Can you find the two keys that will open the lava gates? If you can work out the answer, multiply the two numbers together and turn to that entry.

If you can't solve the puzzle, turn to **73**.

Back on the stairs, the alarm has stopped. From above, you hear distant shouts and thumps but all seems to be quiet below. You wind your way quickly down the spiral steps, listening hard.

"*What are you going to do when you get to the bottom?*" says a familiar voice. Boggo is floating in front of you again, grinning.

"Go away Boggo, not now!" you hiss.

Your best friend's ghost looks hurt. "*I know what's down these stairs,*" he says. "*But I'll only tell you if you're nice to me. Are you sad I'm dead?*"

Suddenly it all comes back to you, and you remember his body hitting the ground. "I... yes of course I am," you stutter.

"*Lovely!*" he says. "*Three guards. That's what's down there. They're stopping every goblin and locking 'em in a room. Maybe you want to try a different route, eh?*"

You look around. You're about two thirds of the way down the tower. The nearest door leads into the picture gallery. You've never seen it before – maybe there's another way out through there? Or maybe you should just carry on – it might be easier to stay hidden if you're among all the other goblins...

If you want to carry on down the stairs, turn to **129**.

If you want to try the picture gallery, turn to **336**.

As Iron Mane sweeps around in a wide turn, the lizardfolk drag their catapult around to follow you. The flaming missile is already loaded, and some of them are furiously cranking back the wire so that it can fire again. But before the lizardfolk can shoot, the iron horse swoops

in, points a hoof and fires an arc of lightning that strikes the tip of the firebolt. There's a huge explosion and a torrent of streaking green fire swallows you up as you wing away from the crater where the war machine once stood. Iron Mane spins wildly out of control and you barely cling on as your shirt is burned from your back.

Deduct 3 LIFE points and turn to **274**.

87

You walk across the balcony. Behind you, the spidery plants are rustling, although there's no breeze. The body is beside the largest pot – a poor dead goblin whom you don't recognise. He's wearing the uniform of the garden staff, and there are big bite marks all over him. He seems to be clutching something in his hand. Every second is precious, so you need to decide what to do, fast.

To search the body, turn to **192**.

To try to find a way off the balcony, turn to **4**.

88

Pulling as hard as you can does no good – you need to find a little more force. So you climb up above the bellows onto the platform where the great iron anvil gleams. It's quite a long drop, but you launch yourself anyway, trying to land feet first directly on the rim of the bellows and push them down. Your plan works a bit too well – the ancient leather gives way beneath your perfectly judged leap, then bounces straight back up, launching you into the air like a rubber ball. You come down hard on your head.

Deduct 1 WITS point and 1 LIFE point.

"*Well that's certainly one way to do it!*" chortles Boggo.

Turn to **237**.

89

You stare at the ruins for a long time as the ghostly old buildings shiver in and out of view, sometimes obscured by the steam from the lava. Your eyes swim and your head aches, but you can't work out the right route. Still you stare, even as Boggo starts to fidget and mumble. After a while he disappears back up the corridor behind you. Another long while passes as you slip into a kind of trance and continue to gaze in frustration at the streets, until you hear a horrified shriek from Boggo somewhere back in the corridors. You soon find out what caused it, as the first of Darkmoon's guard-ghouls slink up to the precipice and hurl you gleefully over the edge.

"WHAT?" cries the lizard in blue. "Do they not know the terms of our contract? No FACES! DARKMOON himself has sworn this! WHERE IS YOUR COMMANDING OFFICER?"

He doesn't thank you, but stalks across to the hobtoads, shouting and waving his arms around. The nervous guards call for their officer who comes in from the staircase outside. Her throat puffs out like a balloon as she starts croaking back.

With everyone's attention on the shrieking, you slip out of the room and down the stairs. Grinning at how you manipulated the lizards, you soon arrive in the banqueting hall of the tower. It has marble floors, a lofty ceiling and is currently full of panicked creatures running about. No one is sure what's going on, but all the goblins are being rounded up. That's not good.

Someone starts shouting. "NO! YOU AIN'T GETTING ANY OF MY POT-GOBS! HOW'M I MEANT TO GET AN ARMY FED IF YOU TAKE THE GOBLINS AWAY? GO BOTHER SOMEONE ELSE INSTEAD, YOU SLACK-WITTED BAWGAWS!"

The voice is unmistakable. It can only belong to Groucho, the fearsome ogre head of the vast tower kitchens. It sounds like he isn't letting the soldiers in to take away his goblins, which means that right now the kitchen is a good place for you to be. You grab a tray of glasses that someone's left on a table and set off across the hall. No one bats an eyelid as you approach the kitchen door. With a final curse, Groucho turns away from the hobtoad guards.

"No one's taking my pot-gobs today!" he shouts.

You breathe a sigh of relief and slip into the kitchen behind him.

Gain 1 ABILITY point and turn to **222**.

91

You feel a muscle pop in your leg as you haul on the brake, but it does no good. The cart isn't slowing down. You're about to go over the edge.

"*Jump!*" shouts Boggo. "*It's your only chance!*"

To let go and jump, turn to **271**.

To keep trying to stop the minecart, turn to **236**.

92

As the hobtoad pins you down and calls for help, you hear a sigh of disappointment echo in your mind.

"*I had such high hopes for you, ringbearer,*" says a strange, deep voice that you don't recognise. "*You fell at the first hurdle – and to a hobtoad of all things! Out of all the miserable creatures, perhaps only the goblin is worse! I will have to find another champion more worthy of the burden of my ring.*"

You wonder who's talking, but you never get to find out as the guards arrive and throw you off the top of the tower.

93

You leap and land with a soft squelch on the other side of the pond – but you haven't quite jumped far enough. Your foot just catches the edge of the poison water and the pain is immediate and intense. The relentless suit of armour doesn't jump after you but plods straight into the bright green liquid. Its legs start to fizz and melt at once, and within seconds it's chest-deep and sinking fast. White smoke fills the air as the metal burns, until only a single metal hand remains above the water, still groping for you until it disappears with a final fizz.

Breathing hard, you limp on your way.

Deduct 2 LIFE points and turn to **204**.

94

Once you've freed yourself from the giant plant's jaws, and backed away, the other plants fall still again, rustling their leaves ever so slightly. You stare around the balcony – you need to find a way off it, and fast.

Turn to **4**.

95

The next few moments are a blur. Surrounded by a crowd of excited people, you are propelled in the darkness down a long, sloping corridor and out into the biggest cave you've ever seen, which is surprisingly well lit by the glowing moss on the ceiling. Lots of brightly coloured tents are in the middle, and the raucous mob is taking you in that direction. Everyone around you keeps repeating the word "ringbearer" as if it's a miracle. Somewhere along the way someone shoves something into your hand, and glancing down you see that it's a silver charm. You're still staring at the charm, which is decorated with the owl face of Tilona the goblin Goddess of Luck, when the crowd parts and a woman's voice pierces the sudden silence. She speaks quietly, but she sounds excited.

"Is it really true?" she says. She looks old and she's wrapped in a rough, homespun shawl but she holds herself very upright and is clearly the leader of the rebels. You nod in answer to her question, and cheers break out as she ushers into you into her tent.

Add the SILVER CHARM to your LOG BOOK. If you fail a skill roll, you can use the charm to reverse the result and succeed instead. You can only use it once – delete it from your LOG BOOK afterwards.

Turn to **249**.

96

You finally cut one of the creature's legs away and it falls to the ground. As you start to back away, it suddenly slashes at you, ripping a hole in your pack and sending your belongings tumbling. Before you can gather them all up, one of them has been swallowed by the marsh.

Choose one item in your LOG BOOK and delete it, then turn to **51**.

97

The voice doesn't speak again, but you feel a prickle on the back of your neck as you walk on, as if something is watching you. You turn and look behind you, but there's nothing to be seen except the silent trees. When you turn to face forwards again, you spot a thin, spindly creature running towards you. It looks like a deer and it's galloping very fast, making a wailing noise. It's only when it's almost on top of you that you realise it's not a normal deer – it's made of branches and vines.

To defend yourself against the wooden beast, turn to **305**.

To try to calm the creature instead, turn to **69**.

98

The hog catches you a glancing blow that sends you sprawling. You can't win this fight, so you scramble up a tree to escape. The angry beast squeals furiously, pacing around the trunk and jabbing it with her tusks. It seems like a very long time before she finally gives up and trots off into the forest. Feeling lucky to be alive, you creep down and set off into the forest again, treading as quietly as possible and checking over your shoulder.

Deduct 1 SNEAK point, then turn to **82**.

Pretending to be interested in a pile of boxes, you eavesdrop on a small group of rebels.

"Sid said there's thousands of 'em in that wizard's army," growls a bearded man with a furrowed brow. "How many are we? Hundreds at most! And all we've got is some fool's prophecy."

"Prophecy? Pah!" The woman next to him nods towards the large red tent. "I thought the lady would protect us, but there's nothing she can do. We should've left when we had a chance. Now we're trapped in this stupid cave."

"Are we all going to die here?" asks a young man, still a boy really. The others exchange glances and one of them pats his shoulder, but his question is left hanging in the air.

To try to reassure them, turn to **316**.

To head to the uniform tent to look for a disguise, turn to **190**.

100

You turn and dash blindly into the forest. Brambles and vines grab you and roots try to trip you up. You're running as fast as you can, but the monster is crashing closer and closer, still roaring. The ground suddenly drops away and you tumble down a steep slope, before smashing into a tree trunk at the bottom.

Deduct 1 LIFE point.

The monster is rushing down the hill towards you. It might have been a brown bear once, but now it's a nightmare vision, with mad eyes raging out of the black mould that covers its body. You have nowhere left to run and you're reaching for the ring when an enormous foot emerges from the forest and stomps down on the bear, pinning it to the ground with earth-shaking force.

"DO NOT USE THAT THING," booms the tree dragon. "DARKMOON'S SORCERY IS THE CAUSE OF OUR CURSE."

It gently lifts its foot away from the bear, which now lies, quite dead, on the forest floor. Then it bends its huge head low over the body and begins to weep. Each time one of its heavy tears splashes onto the bear, wildflowers bloom. The dragon cries until the body is covered in a thick carpet of blossoms, then it folds itself upright again and thunders back towards the road.

"COME WITH ME," it says. It doesn't seem you have a choice.

Turn to **146**.

101

You slink into Blackwell along a side street. The paint on the houses is peeling and many of the buildings are abandoned. You're halfway through the village when you hear galloping hooves on the road behind you. Ducking behind a water barrel, you keep watch. A group of soldiers on horseback thunders into view, all wearing black and heavily armoured. As they pass your hiding place a voice whispers in your ear.

"Can I ask a favour, old friend?"

You nearly jump out of your skin.

"Boggo!" you hiss. "Don't sneak up on me like that."

"Sorry. Was just... wonderin' if you'd mind swinging by my parents' house while you were in town. Just quick, like. I wouldn't mind seeing them... y'know?"

Dozens of riders have dismounted in the village square and are barging into people's homes. From the shouted orders and smashing noises, you know that they're searching for you and that they seem to have the place surrounded. You would have to get past them to reach Boggo's parents' house, and every moment you spend here increases the danger you're in. You look at Boggo, who says nothing further and just looks back at you calmly.

To try to sneak past the soldiers to visit Boggo's parents,

turn to **226**.

To find a way to leave the village as quickly as possible, turn to **151**.

102

The Map Room is silent apart from a fire crackling in the hearth. In the sudden quiet, you can hear your pulse hammering in your ears. Most of the room is taken up by a table with a large map spread out across it, showing the land around Darkmoon's tower. Antique weapons and hunting trophies are displayed on the wall. Boggo is floating in mid-air with a cheeky grin. He looks surprisingly cheerful.

"Now then," he says. *"I'm dead. You ain't. So how are you going to keep it that way?"*

You haven't had time to think about it, but he's right. You need a plan.

"*Here's what I'd do,*" says Boggo. He points at the map. "*You need to take that ring you've stolen to those rebels in Crow Cave. You can warn them that Darkmoon knows where they are – and maybe use the ring to help them fight against him.*"

He never made this much sense when he was alive. Your surprise must show because he gives a little shrug and says: "*Things seem obvious when you're dead.*"

"It is a good plan," you murmur, glancing down at the map. "Not an easy journey though." You stare at the illustrations of swamps and forests and rivers and try not to imagine what kind of monsters might be hiding in them... not to mention Darkmoon's armies.

"*Hmm,*" murmurs Boggo, warming to his new role as your adviser. "*Wonder if there's something that could help you in that map, eh?*"

Turn to **53**.

103

"I'm a friend," you start to say – but the father's angry laugh stops you.

"No goblin can be our friend," he snarls. "Now walk on."

Keeping out of range of his staff, you walk past the silent family. The children watch you, wide-eyed and terrified.

"I hope you get your fire lit," you say, but receive no answer. Soon the family are out of sight and the path starts to climb higher. There are fewer trees here so you can't help worrying about being spotted.

Turn to **34**.

104

You head down the stairs into the cellar. Just as Midge said, the way to go is obvious – a cobbled corridor that runs between the tangle of dark corners and musty storerooms. There isn't anyone about. It's easy to imagine the hobtoads, ghouls and lizardfolk charging about the huge tower just above your head – all of them looking for you. You jog a little faster.

"*Ahem,*" Boggo coughs, as he appears beside you. "*I've been doing a spot of thinking again.*"

"It's becoming a habit, Boggo," you say.

He grins. It's almost as if he's really there, only you can see the wall behind him through his chest.

"*It's about the ring. It's why you can see me, yeah?*"

"That makes sense."

"*Right. But it's also why I can see YOU. Why I can visit, I mean. It tugs me in. Your power, that is. I reckon I won't be the only one, either. You seen any other ghosts?*"

"No, not yet..." That's quite a worrying idea.

"*Well, be ready for that. But the power! If you could see what I see, you'd understand. You're shining all over like a midsummer beacon, and there's a... a STRENGTH to you. It's like you're this storm cloud ready to THUNDERBOOM!*"

You aren't sure if that's worrying or exciting. Probably both.

"*Thing is, I reckon you might be able to USE all that power,*" says Boggo. "*Have a bit of cheeky fun, eh? And stay alive and get your revenge on Darkmoon, of course.*"

The idea of a goblin using one of the legendary ancient artifacts makes you smile. They're famously powerful. The stories say they were forged by gods and wielded by the bravest heroes and wickedest villains in history – the most powerful thing a goblin ever got to wield in those tales was a spade. You're suddenly aware of the frightening weight of the ring in your pocket.

"I'm not a wizard," you say. "I don't even know where to start – let alone what words to say."

"*It doesn't work like that,*" says Boggo. But his ghost is growing fainter. "*You just...*" But he disappears before he can finish the sentence, and the end of the tunnel is approaching. Just as Midge warned, there are three burly hobtoads blocking your path. They've seen you coming, and they're ready.

"Turn back goblin!" shouts one. "No one's leaving the castle today. That's orders."

To attack the hobtoads, turn to **243**.

To try and use the ring to help you, turn to **289**.

105

The cabin door creaks as you edge it open. You peep inside, and immediately panic: a giant hog is squatting there right beside the door. For a moment you stare into its tiny, mad eyes, then it squeals with anger and charges.

GIANT HOG

Rounds: 2   Damage: 2

YOU

If you defeat the hog, turn to **72**.

If you lose, turn to **98**.

106

"*You can't stay here forever,*" says Boggo.

He's right... but your eye is caught by the antique weapons arranged on the wall. They look rather fancy – and powerful too.

Boggo's floating by the open window now. "*There's some vines you could climb down here.*"

If you want to take the time to steal a weapon, turn to **295**.

If you want to climb out of the window on the vines, turn to **168**.

If you want to use the staircase to escape, turn to **62**.

107

It takes all your weight to drag the lever back. The metal shrieks as the speeding wheels try to change tracks, and then there's a heavy clunk and you're shooting off down a different tunnel, zipping past doors and mineshafts.

Boggo whistles. *"Nearly gave me a heart attack!"* he says. *"Although I guess that wouldn't be such a problem now..."*

Turn to **299**.

108

The guard-ghoul holds his torch high as he examines the bank. You cower down in the boat as his gaze passes right over the tree where you're hiding.

Roll one dice and add your SNEAK level and your WITS level.

If your total is 8 or higher, turn to **149**.

If your total is 7 or lower, turn to **185**.

109

You've never seen a plant move so fast. As you turn to run, you feel its stinking breath right behind you.

Roll one dice and add it to your STRENGTH level.

If your total is 5 or higher, turn to **36**.

If your total is 4 or lower, turn to **315**.

110

As you dive down towards the swarm of bat-riders, a cloud of arrows fizzes up to meet you. Most of them clatter against Iron Mane's metal skin, but one slices across your leg, cutting quite deep.

Lightning sparks from the horse's hooves as it slams into the riders. The bats that it strikes fall from the sky immediately, and the other riders dive away, scattering like seeds on the wind as they flee for safety. In the suddenly empty sky, you turn your attention to the battlefield below.

Deduct 2 LIFE points and 1 STRENGTH point and turn to **119**.

111

You keep winding your way down the secret staircase. As far as you can tell, no one has been down here for a very long time. That suspicion is confirmed when you come into a larger chamber inside the walls and find your way blocked by a huge tangle of spiderwebs. Dimly lit, it disappears up into the darkness above you. There's no easy path through the dusty strands of spider's silk.

To push through the web, turn to **342**.

To try to pick your way through the web without disturbing it, turn to **228**.

112

Your eyes flick from shelf to shelf and you quickly gather up all the ingredients and put them in your basket.

"*Look!*" says Boggo. "*I always wanted to try one of these.*" He's pointing at a small pile of Golden Nutmeg Beetles.

"One of those is worth more than my house," you say. "I'm not going to steal it."

"*When you've already stolen the Night Ring?*" snorts Boggo. "*You can't make things much worse.*"

It's hard to argue with this logic so you take a beetle and pop it in your mouth. There's a spicy crunch, and then a flood of rich, velvety goodness, which you can still taste as you hurry back to Groucho with the ingredients. He slaps you on the head for not bringing them faster, and you duck through the cellar door into the silence beyond.

Gain 1 ABILITY point and 1 LIFE point and turn to **104**.

113

You hack at the orb and slice a piece of it away, but your arm nearly becomes stuck inside the gloop and it keeps squelching towards you, trying to sit on you and suck you in. Grimly determined, you stand your ground and fight.

ORB

Rounds: 6   Damage: 1

YOU

If you win, turn to **58**.
If you lose, turn to **217**.

You've barely begun moving across the roof before the bat-riders spot you. You hear a faint, triumphant shout and start to run, as a high-pitched shrieking fills your ears – the bat's death-song is something you never wanted to hear.

You sprint across the tiles. The chimneys and the safety of the door are tantalisingly close – just a few more steps – and you're daring to think that you just might make it. You risk a glance behind you...

It's the last glance you'll ever take. The bat is right at your heels, and its rider pins you to the roof with her spear. Your body is left there for several days, as a warning to others.

115

You don't have to go far before you spot a strange figure lounging on a step overlooking the arena. It looks like the ghost of a lizard-woman. She has fancy clothes and a feather in her cap, and as you come closer you see that she's playing with a dice, making it dance across her knuckles and spin between her fingers.

"*I just wanted to wish you luck, ringbearer,*" the ghost grins. "*I had your quest once – only I didn't quite make it to the end. I never did light that forge. The reason is over there...*" She points across the arena and you see the skeleton of a huge monster with many legs. "*Five hundred years my body has been in the belly of that beast. It swallowed me whole."*

"So you carried the ring too?" you ask.

She nods. *"There have been many of us. Many ringbearers. Be careful, goblin – that ring didn't save any of the others, and it didn't save me when the beast devoured me. But maybe you're luckier than me, eh? Shall we find out? My dice can reveal much about your past and future."* She hands you the dice with a grin, and you roll it on the sand.

Roll one dice and subtract your RING SCORE.

If your total is 3 or higher, turn to **281**.

If your total is 2 or lower, turn to **260**.

116

You scrunch your eyes shut and hold your nose. Somehow, you keep your volcanic sneeze bottled up inside. Meanwhile, just above you, the search is continuing – you hear more shouting and banging as they turn the room upside down – until finally the front door slams shut and all is silent.

Boggo sticks his head through the floor. *"Thank you mate. I owe you more than ever."*

"Don't worry," you say. "Least I can do."

"My folks don't have much," says Boggo. *"But I'm sure they won't miss a bottle of Mum's Magma Sauce. Why don't you grab one? It's really, really good. Bit on the hot side. I can see a couple over there."*

"When are they going to let me out?" you ask, taking the bottle that Boggo is pointing at.

"I think my dad's got a plan," he says.

Before he can explain what it is, a hatch opens in the floor of the smuggler's hole. Dim light streams in from below, along with the dank smell of the river.

"Drop down, friend," whispers Boggo's dad.

You roll across to the hatch. Looking down, you see he's floating in a small, sturdy boat.

"Let's get you away from here," he says.

Add MAGMA HOT SAUCE to your LOG BOOK

and turn to **313**.

II7

You somehow stay just out of reach of the fanged flowers while slashing at their leathery tendrils. Soon, streaks of orange sap spatter your green skin. Luckily, the two plants are too greedy – they lunge for your neck at the same time, and when you duck out of the way they sink their teeth into each other instead of you. Both of them thump to the ground.

After that, the others keep their distance. You waste no time in knotting a few tubes together to make a rope, then you sling it over the side of the balcony and climb down the wall. It's an ankle-breaking drop, so you're pleased you didn't try to jump.

Gain 1 ABILITY point and turn to **302**.

118

The soldier is far too distracted by the struggling child to notice you slipping past – but you can't help feeling like you should've tried to help her. You can hear the shouts of frightened goblins echoing all over the village – and you know you can't do anything to help them either.

Deduct 1 WITS point.

"If I hadn't stolen the ring, none of this would be happening," you mutter.

"Don't worry about it," whispers Boggo. *"If you hadn't stolen it, you couldn't take it to the rebels either. Now come on, follow me."*

Turn to **9**.

119

From high above, in the early evening light, you can see the battlefield spread out beneath you like a map, with Darkmoon's army arranged in long lines. Great regiments of spear-soldiers are marching forwards. A steady thump comes from the ogre drummers pounding their cavernous drums, and further back lizardfolk are using giant catapults to fling balls of fire that arc high and fall on the rebels. It's hard not to be frightened by the sheer numbers of the enemy. There are thousands upon thousands of hobtoads, skeletons, minotaurs... and of course goblins. As Iron Mane sweeps high above them all, you suddenly realise that you surely know some of the tiny figures down there. Some of those are goblins you've feasted and gambled and joked with, and most of them aren't bad – they're just like you, really, taking the work and glad for the pay and a roof for their family. Your mind turns back to the many times a human has cheated you, or insulted you to your face – and the rebels are humans for the most part. Why exactly are you trying to save them?

"*A change of heart?*" says the Smith, reading your thoughts. "*Maybe it's time to give those fools up? They seem to have little hope of succeeding anyway, even with brave Iron Mane helping.*"

You look at the tiny rebel army. Clustered together on a hill, they look like a pebble trying to stand firm against an ocean wave. You see humans and minotaurs and other beasts standing together, shield to shield, and you remember what their courage stands for: the end of Darkmoon's cruelty.

"No," says Boggo. "No backing down now. We're going to kill that wizard. Well, you are. I'm going to watch."

You wish you had Boggo's certainty, but you're glad he's still around. You open your mouth to reply, but your thoughts are scattered by a sudden roar from the Smith.

"*HOLD TIGHT!*" he bellows.

Out of the corner of your eye, you see a flaming green missile speeding towards you – a magical weapon conjured to knock you from the sky. Iron Mane dives out of the way, spiralling down as the missile bends its track to follow. The sudden swerve sends you flying out of the saddle, with your legs trailing behind you. All that's keeping you from falling is your slippery grip on the reins, which are stretched tight.

"*LET GO!*" shouts the Iron Smith. "*YOU MUST LET GO!*" But as you glimpse the rocky ground far below, your every instinct is screaming at you to keep holding on.

To keep hold of the reins and try to haul yourself back into the saddle, turn to **47**.

To trust the Smith and let go, turn to **337**.

120

You reach the bottom of the stairs at last. You're in a small, dark chamber with a simple wooden door ahead of you. Faint light gleams through the keyhole and around the edges of the boards. You pause at the door, listening: you hear chatter, shouted orders, dishes clattering, wooden platters being stacked. It can only be the tower's kitchen. You test the handle, then edge the door open.

Turn to **222**.

121

"I'm not giving you anything," you say. "I can't believe you'd betray one of your own." The girl stares at you, open-mouthed. "Go on then," you say. "Shout. Alert all the guards."

"Well, well, well!" she says eventually, breaking into a grin and with a new respect in her voice. "A goblin with a bit of courage.

Well, I won't stand in your way and here's a free bit of advice. Maybe you've guessed Blackwell's surrounded, which means the only way you're getting out is the river. I'd head to the jetty and steal a boat if I was you."

You give her a silent nod of thanks and turn to leave.

"Wherever you're headed," she says quietly as you walk away, "I hope you get there before they do."

Gain 1 ABILITY point and turn to **195**.

122

"Fits perfectly!" Boggo giggles as you pull on the hat and the bells jingle.

"Why did I listen to you?" you say, looking down at yourself.

Boggo's pale grin gleams in the shadows. *"You'll blend right in! Just remember to dance like a proper jester, and nobody will know the difference."*

Unable to tell if this is a genius idea or a terrible one, you take a deep breath and step out into the cave, trying to caper like a jester. As Boggo predicted, no one seems to takes any notice – they're too busy looking worried and talking in low voices. Feeling more and more self-conscious, you dance a few steps as you cross the cave, and your bells jingle brightly again. The sound makes a burly otterling turn to look at you. He tilts his head, studying you carefully, then leaps high in the air, landing neatly in front of you and pointing his finger dramatically at your hat. He speaks in a high-pitched voice that carries clearly over the hubbub.

"Halt, goblin! Your jester's garb fools no one!"

The crowd falls silent and you freeze, unsure how to reply, as the otterling slowly reaches out a single claw and tugs your hat off. A gasp goes up all around you and several creatures draw their weapons. There's no escaping this, so you let yourself be led away by the otterling to a heavily guarded tent with an officer sitting at a table outside it, writing a letter.

"I've a caught a goblin spy sir," says the otterling, sounding pleased. The officer looks up, his pen still hovering over the paper.

"This jester? A spy? What were they thinking?" He grabs you by the shoulder and pushes you into the tent.

Lose 1 SNEAK point and turn to **328**.

123

You run even faster, although your lungs are burning. Up ahead, you've spotted a pair of rocks that you might be able to stretch your rope between. If the suit of armour walks into it, maybe it can be stopped... but can you get it tied up in time?

Roll one dice and add it to your WITS level.

If your total is 6 or higher, turn to **233**.

If your total is 5 or lower, turn to **138**.

You jump forwards just in time. A torrent of flame roars out of the dragon's mouth and fills the staircase behind you. Shaking, you examine yourself – the toe of your left boot is singed, but you seem to be in one piece.

Turn to **111**.

125

"Alright," you say. "I'll do it."

"*You're a wonder, chum!*" says Stinker. "*It's a real simple job, right – except, you have to remember it's also really dangerous here, so you're going to have to follow my instructions exactly or you'll die, and I won't get my skull back.*"

This mission is starting to sound less appealing. As you wonder how you can back out of it, the banner overhead shivers in the breeze. Its colours are faded, but once upon a time it was probably purple and gold.

"What's the deal with all the flags?" you ask.

"*They mark where a knight was buried,*" says Stinker. "*A lot of fancy folk in shiny armour died in the battle. They got proper burials, unlike us poor goblins. Couldn't even get my skull back, could I? Condemned to stalk this marsh until a kind soul restored it to me. That kind soul being you...*"

"Alright Stinker, tell me what I have to do," you mutter.

"*Start at the shattered tree. Then walk a dozen paces north till you reach the remains of an iron soldier. Go east until you reach the ruined tower, then circle counter-clockwise around it till you reach the path. Don't go clockwise or you'll end up dead. Walk north to the big crater and then strike out east. Stop at the poisoned marsh and head north till you reach the giant skeleton of the behemoth. Are you getting all this?*"

"Yes," you reply. "I think so."

"*Good, alright. From the behemoth strike out east again, and you should reach a war chariot. Now head south to the pond. Do not put a foot in the water but head west towards my frozen companions. If you touch them, they'll never let go, so best avoid that. Head south until you reach the great cannon. You're nearly there now! A dozen paces east and you reach a grassy knoll. Walk to the top and then due south. You'll find my helmet and my skull just there.*"

Look at the map on the next page, and follow the goblin's instructions. Count the number of funeral flags that you pass under while on the route. Multiply that number by 21 and turn to that entry.

If you can't find the skull, turn to **201**.

126

"*HOLD ON!*" shouts the Iron Smith. Your blade is above your head, and Iron Mane judges its flight perfectly, letting you slice across the leather straps that hold the castle in place on the elephant's back. Somehow the Smith's magic is flowing through your arm and your weapon cuts through the metal and thick leather as if it was all made of paper. The sudden release of tension sends the severed straps of the harness whipping about like angry snakes. One of them slaps you in the back of the head, and you fall from the saddle, tumbling and bouncing away from the elephant's maddened feet. The great beast rears up as the harness slips from its back and the castle structure smashes to the ground, splintering into a hundred pieces. Suddenly free, the elephant charges wildly through the enemy soldiers.

All around you, the battle stops. Everyone, rebels and enemies alike, is staring at the ruined castle.

Your ears are ringing and you can hardly believe you're alive. High overhead you can see Iron Mane turning, perhaps looking for you. A fire has broken out in the remains of the castle. For a long moment, time seems to stand still as thousands of eyes gaze into the flaming wreckage. Then you spot a dark figure climbing out of it, moving slowly and calmly through the flames as if they weren't hot at all.

Turn to **61**.

127

The smuggler's hole is damp and smells of fish and pepper. You scrunch yourself into a tiny ball among all the boxes and jars and bottles, trying to stay absolutely silent. Above, you hear the scrape of the chest being dragged back on top of the trapdoor, and the next moment there's a lot of banging and shouting as the soldiers storm in. Their heavy boots rumble right overhead, then there's a smashing sound and Boggo's mum starts shrieking. When she eventually stops, everything seems to be quiet up there... but you haven't heard the front door so the soldiers must still be in the house. Suddenly, your nose starts to tickle. Pepper always makes you want to sneeze, and you can feel a huge one building inside you. Wincing, you desperately try to hold it in.

Roll one dice and add it to your STRENGTH level.

If your total is 5 or higher, turn to **116**.

If your total is 4 or lower, turn to **296**.

128

The griefers close in on you in a frenzied whirl of claws, slobbering jaws and high-pitched giggling. Each one wants to claim the prize of killing you, so you must fight them one at a time.

If you lose a round, add together the damage ratings of the remaining griefers, then deduct the total from your LIFE points. If a griefer is dead, don't add their damage rating. If you win a round, deduct the COMBAT points only from the griefer you chose to attack. And remember to keep a note of how many rounds you have left for that griefer too.

GRIEFER 1

Rounds: 3   Damage: 1

GRIEFER 2

Rounds: 3   Damage: 1

GRIEFER 3

Rounds: 4   Damage: 1

YOU

If you win, turn to **298**.

If you lose, turn to **321**.

129

As you hurry around the corner, you almost crash into three hobtoad guards who are blocking the stairs.

"In there, goblin," one grunts, pointing to an open door.

"Orders are – everyone's to be locked up."

You hesitate for a second, weighing up your options – but you wouldn't beat them in a fight and you'll never talk your way past them either, so you do as you're told.

Turn to **173**.

130

You approach the snail with soft steps and its rancid smell fills your throat and nose. It's chewing steadily on the body of a large, frog-like creature.

Roll one dice and add it to your SNEAK level.

If your total is 8 or higher, turn to **335**.

If your total is 7 or lower, turn to **44**.

131

The minotaur steps in and slices you in half with a single sweep of her scythe. Your broken body topples onto the iron steps.

"*Welcome to the long undeath, goblin,*" says the minotaur wearily. "*By the light of the Goddess, may the next ringbearer be a more worthy vessel.*"

132

Several times, the ghoul's razor-sharp blade whistles through the air and comes perilously close to cutting your head off, but you dance out of the way. Eventually it grows frustrated and swings at you wildly, and you take your chance. Rolling under its outstretched arm, you kick its leg as hard as you can and it topples into the river. Its armour drags it deep beneath the surface, and you duck down quickly to untie a rowing boat. Slipping into it, you push out onto the dark water. Behind you, Blackwell village burns.

Gain 1 ABILITY point and turn to **178**.

133

"*You have resisted the urge to use my gift,*" says the voice. "*Such discipline is admirable – I see why my ring chose you. So here, please accept my blessing.*" You feel a calming warmth spread through your body, as if a gentle hand was polishing away every ache and pain, one by one.

Add 3 LIFE points.

"*Now for the true test,*" says the voice. "*You must travel to my forge in the city below and light the furnace – and you must do it without the help of the ring.*"

"Hold on," you say. "Why do I have to light a forge?"

"*Because then I come into my full power, and I can help you win your battle, ringbearer. But hurry – your enemies are not far behind you...*" The voice fades and you stand there, listening to the darkness. Somewhere down there, the Iron Smith is waiting for you. But he's clearly not alone – from the depths far below, you hear something roaring...

Turn to **26**.

134

Your fingers start to blister on the metal and the boiling vapours of the lava are almost making you pass out.

Deduct 1 LIFE point.

You know that if you don't climb back onto the top of the bridge, you're going to plummet to a fiery death. Gasping, you heave yourself over the iron railing, feeling terribly exposed.

Roll one dice and add it to your SNEAK level.

If your total is 7 or higher, turn to **301**.

If your total is 6 or lower, turn to **348**.

135

Marcox eyes you coldly. "What's happening up there, goblin?" he asks quietly.

You stare up at his dead eyes and the grey skin stretched tight across his skull. You open your mouth to reply, but it's hard to lie with those eyes boring into your brain.

Roll one dice and add it to your STRENGTH level and your WITS level.

If your total is 5 or higher, turn to **10**.

If your total is 4 or lower, turn to **206**.

You give him a quick nod, and hurry past.

"Well! Suit yourself then, Tower slave," he snaps. "A magpie's curse on a goblin with no manners."

As he mutters those words, you feel a sudden heaviness sink into your bones – the farmer has put a goblin hex on you. You hurry away before anything worse happens.

Deduct 1 SNEAK point and turn to **147**.

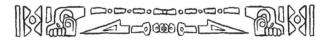

137

It might have been a glint of metal or a flash of wood in the torchlight, but somehow the guard-ghoul spots you. He howls to his oarsmen to stop then points right at your hiding place. There's no way you can escape this, there's no way you can survive... until you remember the ring. Even as you think of it, your hand has reached into your pocket and the ring is already on your finger. Suddenly you see everything very clearly and you know exactly what to do. It's as if the ring is controlling you, not the other way around.

"SINK THEM!" you shout and point at the boat. Instantly, ghostly hands rise from the river and drag the guard-ghoul and the rowers beneath the water. They barely have time to shout out. Boggo's father screams in terror and cowers away from you. Far away, somewhere else, you feel Darkmoon notice what you've done. Sweating and shaking, you pull the ring from your finger, swearing that you'll never use it again.

Fill in the next section of the RING TRACKER on your

LOG BOOK then roll one dice.

If the number is equal to or lower than your new RING SCORE, turn to **268**.

If the number is higher than your RING SCORE, turn to **155**.

138

You loop the rope around the first rock and fasten it with a quick hitch knot, but when you try the same thing on the other side the wet rope slips through your fingers. As you frantically try again, you hear the suit of armour squelching closer and closer through the muck, until it reaches out a metal hand and grabs your shoulder. Jerking yourself free, you drop the rope and run for your life.

Deduct 1 LIFE point, delete the ROPE from your LOG BOOK and turn to **211**.

139

The cat jumps for your throat, hissing like a kettle.

JERVIS THE HOUSE PANTHER

Rounds: 2   Damage: 2

YOU

If you defeat the cat, turn to **85**.

If you lose, turn to **282**.

140

Fighting with your back to the wall, you beat back the snail's tentacles, until you gain enough space to run. The snail roars in anger as you escape, and slithers after you. You run blindly into a bewildering maze of stairs and corridors – soon the snail has no idea where you are, but neither do you...

Turn to **356**.

141

You go in without knocking – this is no time for politeness – and surprise Boggo's parents at their dinner. You've only met them once before, but they recognise you right away. They also seem to guess that you're in trouble.

"What can we do to help?" asks Boggo's dad.

"Something happened at the Tower," says his mum, without taking her eyes off you. You can see the fear in them.

"It's..." You don't know how to say it. "He's..."

"Boggo..." says his mum.

"Darkmoon killed him," you blurt out. "Boggo did nothing wrong. And he just murdered him."

For a couple of seconds, the two old goblins stare at you, their faces frozen, as though they haven't heard what you said. Then they slowly slump together and hug each other tight. Boggo drifts across the room and puts his arms around them, though they have no idea he's there. Everyone is crying, including you.

"You did a proper job, coming to tell us," says Boggo's dad finally, wiping his eyes. "He always said you were a true friend."

Before you can say any more, the soldiers' shouts are right outside, and the heartbroken goblins see your look of terror. Boggo's mum jumps across the room and pushes a heavy chest aside. Moving just as quickly, her husband jerks up the trapdoor that was hidden beneath it.

"Smuggler's hole. Get inside," he says, pointing to the dark space under the floorboards. You jump in, just in time.

Turn to **127**.

142

Inch by inch, intensely aware of the huge bulk of the dragon and the heat of its breath hissing across the cobblestones, you tiptoe past it. To your relief, it doesn't stir.

Turn to **218**.

143

"I promise I'm friendly," you plead.

"Don't move!" shouts the father. The children are cowering behind their mother's skirts and you wonder what terrible stories they've been told about wicked goblins.

"I'm trying to find Crow Cave," you say. The humans look surprised when you mention the name, and the mother's face softens slightly. Pressing on before they have time to reconsider, you continue: "I have a message to deliver, and I'm being hunted by Darkmoon. Please, please help me."

The father scowls and is about to shout at you again when his wife calls out.

"Take the first turning on the right, by the aspen tree just up that hill. It's a shortcut to the caves. You'll see the entrance above the waterfall."

"Mariam!" growls the father. "You can't trust a goblin!"

"I trust this one," she says quietly, continuing to look you in the eyes as her husband shakes his head.

"Thank you," you say and scamper up the hill. One of the children smiles at you as you go past.

Turn to **341**.

144

You and the girl drag the unconscious soldier into an alleyway. For a moment you both stand there, breathing heavily. From all around you come the sounds of the search – more soldiers have arrived and you can smell the dirty smoke of burning buildings. The girl kicks the soldier one more time for good luck. You're glad you saved her.

"Thanks stranger," she says. "You fight good. I'm Eagle. What's your name?"

You don't want to tell her – she'll be safer if she doesn't know. "What's the fastest way to get out of this village?" you ask instead.

"The river – get a boat from the jetty," says Eagle. "D'you want me to show you the way?"

"No," you say. "You've been in enough trouble today. I'll find it."

"Suit yourself," she says and flashes you a grin before running off into the gathering smoke.

"*Come on, you hero,*" says Boggo. "*We're nearly there.*"

Gain 1 ABILITY point and turn to **9**.

145

The nearest plant is twice as tall as you, dark green with huge pink flowers fringed with stabbing teeth. It smells sweet and sickly, like rotten candy. The tube that runs from its pot to the barrel in the corner has an odd glowing liquid seeping out.

To look for a way off the balcony, turn to **4**.

To investigate the body in the corner, turn to **87**.

To investigate the barrel, turn to **293**.

You're walking through the deep tangle of the forest now, well off the path, but the trees and vines and brambles seem to bend around the dragon as it strides forwards, as if it were a fish slicing through the water. When you look back, the forest has closed again behind you.

You come to another dense patch of black rot, with lumpy mushroom growths all over everything.

"THE SOURCE OF THE CURSE LIES SOMEWHERE IN THAT FILTH," booms the dragon. "IT IS DARKMOON'S CURSE. HE SEEKS TO KILL ALL THAT HE CANNOT CONTROL. I HAVE KEPT IT AT BAY AS WELL I CAN, BUT I CANNOT DESTROY IT AT ITS SOURCE."

It looks down at you and its expression is suddenly pleading.

"ONLY YOU CAN DO THAT, YOUNG GOBLIN, WITH YOUR EVIL RING – SO WILL YOU HELP US NOW?"

If you want to help the dragon, turn to **278**.

If you refuse, turn to **244**.

147

Soon enough you see and smell the woodsmoke rising from the cooking fires in Blackwell. The town bell is tolling, calling the goblins in from the fields. As you near the village, you come across a rundown graveyard tucked amongst the trees. Weathered gravestones are dotted about, some well-tended, others long forgotten. You're about to walk past when a voice calls out to you from amongst the graves.

"*Hey! Hey! Ringbearer! Yoohoo!*"

It's not Boggo's voice – so why did they call you Ringbearer?

To investigate the friendly voice, turn to **22**.

To carry on into Blackwell, turn to **101**.

148

Iron Mane slips between the elephant's legs, flying just below the belly straps which hold the castle's great harness in place.

"*SLICE IT AWAY!*" yells the Smith. Your arm is raised high, and you can feel the Smith's strength in it as you prepare to strike. But as you swing at the thick leather your weapon catches and you are ripped from the horse's back and thrown to the ground. Before you can move, one of the elephant's mighty feet has crushed you flat.

149

Crouched beneath the willow and trying not to breathe, you can only wait as the guard-ghoul stares slowly around. After a while, it turns quickly and signals to the oarsmen. The boat splashes onwards, and its drums dim into the distance. Once you think enough time has passed, you untie your boat and push out into the current. You row for several hours, until you arrive beneath the shattered arch of Rocklaw Bridge. You've never been here before, but it's as huge and dramatic as the stories say, towering over the river as if made by a clumsy giant. Jumping ashore, you push the boat out into the river and watch it disappear into the darkness before you climb up the bank. Hopefully no one will ever know you came this way.

Turn to **353**.

150

You deftly climb over the fallen tree, avoiding the black growths that have spread all over it. The stink of death is even stronger when you are right up close. You hold your breath and make it through safely.

Turn to **188**.

"It's just not safe," you say. "I'm sorry Boggo."

"*I understand. No worries*," he murmurs, and fades quickly away.

You definitely don't have time to worry about how he's feeling – the soldiers are rampaging through the village, kicking down doors and shouting at the terrified goblins behind them. There's no obvious way to get past them without being spotted, but at least it's starting to get dark. You stick to the shadows, hoping to avoid attention and get away from the soldiers as quietly as possible. But you aren't sneaky enough to avoid the keen eyes of a goblin girl who's squatting outside her shack, skinning a rabbit.

"Oi stranger!" she calls, and you freeze. She puts down her knife, watching you closely. "Where are you going?"

"Keep quiet," you hiss.

"Suppose this mess is all your fault?" she smiles cheekily. "They're looking for you, aren't they? I could just shout right now and in ten seconds you'd have a dozen soldiers here. Shall I do that? Or are you going to give me something nice to keep quiet?"

To give the goblin girl a bribe to stay quiet, turn to **74**.

If you don't want to give her anything, turn to **121**.

152

You take the weapon down from the wall. Add the item you've chosen to your LOG BOOK. It counts as a weapon so you no longer need to subtract one from your ATTACK rolls. Now roll one dice.

If you roll a 1, 2 or 3, turn to **16**.

If you roll a 4, 5 or 6, turn to **232**.

153

You walk across to the great anvil in the centre of the forge. Beside it rises the furnace, which is now fed by a stream of bubbling lava. All around you, smaller engines are firing up and machines are groaning into life. The air is filled with the whistle of pressurised steam and the thumping of pistons, and as you peer inside the main furnace you see lava surging into it.

"*Only one more task, young goblin!*" says the Smith. "*Now you must summon the wind so that our little blaze here can become an inferno.*"

To one side of the pyramid is a dragonskin bellows with a funnel to shoot air into the heart of the forge. The device is powered by a giant iron arm with a lever next to it. You pull the lever and the iron arm begins to push at the bellows handle – but the hardened skin of its wind-sack won't move. It's stuck fast.

"*Yes,*" murmurs the Iron Smith. "*I suppose it has been a few hundred years since we last fired it up. It may need a bit of unsticking.*"

Try as you might, the bellows won't close, even when you pull down on the handle with all your weight.

Roll one dice and add it to your STRENGTH level.

If your total is 8 or higher, turn to **266**.

If your total is 7 or lower, turn to **88**.

154

As soon as you pull out one of the tubes, all the plants turn to look at you. Suddenly, the nearest one bites down at you with alarming speed. You dodge out of the way and nearly fall into another gaping, flowery mouth.

The plants give little thought to fighting as a group, so if you lose a round, only count the damage from the plant you chose to attack. If you win a round, only deduct the COMBAT points from that plant, too. And remember to keep a note of how many rounds you have left.

CARNIVOROUS PLANT 1

Rounds: 5   Damage: 1

YOU

CARNIVOROUS PLANT 2

Rounds: 5   Damage: 1

YOU

If you win, turn to **117**.

If you lose, turn to **334**.

155

Boggo's dad says nothing as he unties the boat and heads back out into the current. He's shivering and won't look you in the eye. The black water is deep and there's no sign of the boat that you sunk – not even a bubble or a scrap of cloth. You are half-expecting Darkmoon to appear, as he rows you silently down the river but soon you arrive beneath the shattered arch of Rocklaw Bridge. The giant stones nearly block the current, and you can't imagine the force it must have taken to tumble them down.

"Get out of my boat," he says.

"I'm sorry..." you begin.

"Sorcery like that," he gestures at the broken bridge. "It breaks everything. So be careful what you become, goblin. Don't let it break you."

Without another word he unties the boat and rows back upstream, leaving you standing on the bank alone in the darkness.

Turn to **353**.

156

The tomb's door is dizzyingly tall and richly decorated with pictures that seem to show scenes from the Iron Smith's life. Three iron bowls marked KNOWLEDGE, IRON and POWER are placed before it, and there are piles of iron skulls everywhere.

"*He really likes his iron, this guy,*" whispers Boggo.

The voice of the Iron Smith growls in your ear:

"*There are three things I value above all else:*

KNOWLEDGE is born from hammer and bone.

IRON is made from fire and stone.

POWER is forged from spears and thrones.

Do you know what I value? Show me that you do, ringbearer. Count, calculate. And show me your answer in skulls."

You stare at the images, trying to make sense of the Smith's riddle. Look at the picture on the next page. Counting only the images on the door and ignoring items that are on the floor, can you work out how many skulls you need to place in each bowl so that the values of knowledge, iron and power are correct? Put those three numbers together in order, to make a three-digit number, and turn to that entry.

If you can't solve the puzzle, turn to **312**.

Iron Mane sweeps around in a long curve that takes you over the forest at the edge of the battlefield – it must be planning to come at the giant crossbow from behind. Glancing down, you see movement beneath you among the trees, then you realise it's the trees themselves that are moving! Dragging their roots out of the ground, they're striding forward towards Darkmoon's hordes, with mountain bears and packs of wolves running among them. At the head of the forest's charge rumbles the tree dragon itself, shaking the land with each thunderous stomp. As you fly over the war engines, the forest army smashes into the panicking lizardfolk with a great splintering of branches. The machines are overwhelmed by surging vines and toppled to the ground. As your eyes turn to the rest of the battlefield again, you offer a silent prayer of thanks to the tree dragon.

"Where's Darkmoon?" you shout, struggling to hear yourself above the whistling of the wind and the chaos below.

"*He is close now,*" replies the Iron Smith. "*The moment is almost upon us.*"

Turn to **274**.

You clamber away from the cloud of maddened hornets, but you're not nearly fast enough. Some of them swarm after you and begin to attack any patch of exposed skin. Each sting burns like a red-hot needle and you feel fat lumps rising on your neck and hands and ankles, but you've no way of pulling them off or getting away. Somehow, you force yourself to keep climbing down the vines. Below, you can see a large balcony garden filled with plants. Finally, you're close enough to jump onto it and the hornets leave you in peace. You collapse on the ground – everything hurts, but gradually the agony fades to a dull throb.

Deduct 3 LIFE points and turn to **287**.

159

The girl is putting up a good fight against the soldier and you're grateful for the distraction, though you feel guilty for not helping her.

Roll one dice and add it to your SNEAK level.

If your total is 4 or higher, turn to **118**.

If your total is 3 or lower, turn to **223**.

160

The old lady continues to explain that she expects the ringbearer to arrive shortly, but the crowd is becoming more and more bad-tempered. You slip through it, looking for the right person to talk to. Eventually you settle on an elegant old human warrior leaning against a post, twisting his long white beard around his finger. You sidle up to him.

"Excuse me," you say. "Um... I think... I'm the ringbearer."

"Eh? What's that? Have to speak louder, young'un. I'm a bit deaf," he barks, blinking down at you and peering under your hood. Suddenly his eyes go wide. "Hoy! You're a goblin!" Before you can speak, the tip of his dagger is pointing at your belly.

"But I'm the ringbearer," you plead.

"What? Speak louder or I'll stab you one!" he shouts.

"I'M THE RINGBEARER!" you shout back, pulling the ring from your pocket and holding it up. You watch his expression change, anger and suspicion turning to amazement. Without another word, he grabs your arm and guides you through the crowd, pushing people out of the way, to where the old lady is standing on her barrel. Not even pausing to explain anything to her, he hoists you up onto the barrel beside her then shouts:

"AS THE LADY PREDICTED, THE RINGBEARER IS HERE! BEHOLD THE GOBLIN!"

There's a shocked silence, and then everyone starts talking at once. Some people cheer, while others look at you doubtfully and whisper to each other. The old lady stares into your eyes and takes your hand in hers. "It was wise of you to choose General Mumbray as your champion, ringbearer. Not everyone would have believed you. I am glad you have come. I dreamed of you, you know. You are arriving rather later than we might have hoped, but at least you are here."

Unsure what to say to this, you hold out the ring for her to take, but to your surprise she shakes her head.

"No," she says. "It is yours – and your burden to carry."

"But I don't want it!" you say.

"I think that is precisely why it chose you," she says. Then she raises her arms and the raucous crowd falls abruptly silent.

Gain 1 ABILITY point and turn to **242**.

161

"A man in black, eh?" The General nods, as if this confirms his suspicions. He turns to the guards. "It must be that thieving fox

Devrix again! Quick, we've no time to lose!"

The General and the guard-ghouls stomp up the stairs, leaving you free to continue your escape.

Turn to **256**.

162

An argument seems to be simmering among the griefers. The biggest one is charging about shouting, while all the others bicker and grumble as they scramble out of his reach – it looks as if they're all trying to blame each other for some mistake.

"*This is all going to kick off,*" whispers Boggo. "*It just needs a match, and they'll go boom.*"

Inspired by Boggo's advice, you pick up a rock. While the griefers are focused on snapping at each other, you hurl it at the big one. It crunches into the back of his head with a satisfying thunk, and he shrieks in rage and punches his nearest companion into the fire. As soon as he goes down, all the others jump on their fallen friend in a shower of sparks and thrashing limbs. Seizing your opportunity, you slip past. Their roaring and swearing and strange giggling grow ever more savage behind you, but you hardly notice because you're approaching the forge at last.

Gain 1 ABILITY point and turn to **64**.

You tread carefully in the footprints and make it across to the stone basin without triggering any traps. When you stare into the carved nest you see the big glowing egg bobbing just beneath the surface. The glowing green water ripples softly. It looks cool and clear, and smells like summer grass.

If you want to grab the egg, turn to **248**.

If you want to sip the water, turn to **45**.

164

You wake up suddenly a few hours later, with Boggo's dad gently shaking your shoulders. He's tied the boat up underneath an overhanging bank and pulled branches down low to cover it.

"SHH!" he whispers. "They're coming." A drum is beating in the darkness, getting louder and louder by the second, and as you peer between the branches you see a thin boat sweep around the corner. It's lit by flaming torches and a dozen goblin oarsmen are rowing in a frenzy to the beat of the drum. You think they're going to row right past you, but then the guard-ghoul who's steering raises his hand. The goblin on the drums stops and all the oars lift at once, so that the boat is drifting down the river towards your hiding place.

"This isn't good," hisses Boggo's dad.

Roll one dice and add your SNEAK level and your WITS level.

If your total is 8 or higher, turn to **310**.

If your total is 7 or lower, turn to **137**.

165

"I saw a monster up there," you exclaim, wide-eyed. "It looked like...
like a demon!"

Roll one dice, and add it to your WITS level.

If your total is 5 or higher, turn to **311**.

If your total is 4 or lower, turn to **76**.

166

You slip your free hand into your pocket and the ring jumps eagerly
onto your finger. You sense the power surging inside you again: the
feeling is exciting and disturbing.

"LET ME GO," you command. You're not quite sure why you've
said it, but it works like a dream. To your surprise, the ghoul drops
your arm and cowers away as if hearing your voice was painful.

"GO AWAY. NEVER SPEAK OF ME," you order.

The creature flees into the burning village, and you don't wait for
someone else to spot you. Somewhere far away, you feel Darkmoon's
attention switch towards you. Frightened, you pull the ring from your
finger and scamper to the end of the dock. Quickly and quietly, you
untie a rowing boat and push off into the river. The current soon
carries you away from the smoke and screams. You've made it...

Colour in the next section of the RING TRACKER on your LOG
BOOK then roll one dice.

If you roll equal to or lower than your RING SCORE, turn to **6**.

If you roll higher than your RING SCORE, turn to **178**.

167

Your fears are well-founded – the hunters have sniffed out your scent, and even though you untie your boat and row hard down the river in the darkness, they're coming for you now. In the darkness of the river, all is silent apart from the splashing of your oars, and then something catches your eye in the branches that spread above the water – there's someone standing up there. You just have time to realise who it is before pale fire engulfs you and lifts you high into the air.

"I'll have my ring back now, if I may," says Darkmoon, then your body drops like a stone into the icy river.

168

Boggo was right, the thick vines stretching all over the wall aren't difficult to climb. What's tricky instead is the height: the bottom seems very far away, and you try not to think about the drop as you move gradually lower.

"*If only you could fly, eh?*" says Boggo, suddenly bobbing in the air beside you as you clamber down.

"Be quiet!" you hiss. It's almost reassuring how little Boggo has changed since he died – same old chatterbox. He does fall silent now though, which is just as well because it allows you to hear the buzzing noise that's getting louder and louder. You stop and glance down... just in time to avoid putting your foot through a hornets' nest: a cauldron-sized ball of baked mud is stuck to the wall just below you, with big hornets buzzing in and out of holes in its speckled surface.

To stay very still and hope they haven't noticed you, turn to **306**.

To try to climb around the hornet's nest, turn to **59**.

169

You sprint away into the mist but the armour follows, clanking, clanking, clanking. It's surprisingly fast: soon you're panting but its long strides never stop. You aren't going to be able to keep this up forever. You need to either slow it down or escape – but how?

If you have a BLANKET and want to throw it over the suit of armour, turn to **12**.

If you have a ROPE and want to try to trip it up, turn to **123**.

If you have neither or would prefer to keep on running while you think up a plan, turn to **211**.

170

The tree dragon towers above you, and you know you only have seconds to save your life.

"I'm sorry," you beg. "Please. I didn't know what I was doing."

Roll one dice and add it to your WITS level.

If your total is 4 or higher, turn to **25**.

If your total is 3 or lower, turn to **329**.

171

Bracing your legs against the wall and clutching the rope, you begin to make your way down the shaft. But it's a long way in the dark and your legs keep slipping as the rope swings about. Your arms burn with the effort of hanging on, and you're tiring fast. Eventually you lose your grip and fall the rest of the way down, smashing into the little elevator box that's used to carry food.

You pick yourself up, bruised and shaken. You can hear a busy kitchen on the other side of the hatch and you can smell it too – someone is baking a pie. Easing the hatch open, you slip quietly into the room beyond.

Deduct 2 LIFE points and turn to **222**.

172

This time you don't do what Boggo suggests, but you're smart enough to adapt his idea. Why would snails have any interest in a forge? Instead of following the snail trails, you decide to avoid them and it works like a dream: you aren't surprised by any more snails and you soon find yourself in straighter tunnels, which all lead in the same direction. As you go deeper you pass ancient homes and shops and what looks like a theatre – clearly this was once a city carved out of the earth. Sometimes the open spaces are lit by flaming jets of gas, and in the flickering light you try to imagine people living out their lives here. Finally, you emerge into a huge cavern. You're standing right at the top of it, with a precipice dropping away in front of you. As you tiptoe forward and peer over the edge, warm air wafts over your face. Glancing down, you see rivers of red-hot lava weaving through the ruins far below.

Gain 1 ABILITY point and turn to **307**.

173

Half a dozen goblins have already been herded into the room, although you don't recognise any of them. Hundreds of goblins work in the tower every day, which may very slightly increase your chances of blending in and staying alive. A few spindly lizardfolk have also been brought in, wearing their hooded ceremonial masks and sounding rather annoyed to be here. A huge minotaur is grumbling in the corner about how noisy and inconvenient this all is. Everyone is keeping well away from it, even the hobtoad guards.

None of the goblins has any idea what's going on and you find yourself wishing that Boggo would appear – he might have another one of his good ideas. The room is long and wide and has a big table running down the middle – some kind of feasting room, you assume. Stuffed animals, no doubt killed by Darkmoon, stare down at you from the walls.

You're aware that the search is closing in and every second is precious – so how will you escape?

If you want to look for a way out, turn to **327**.

If you want to talk to the lizardfolk, turn to **275**.

If you want to talk to the grumpy minotaur, turn to **37**.

174

As you approach the dock in your disguise, you notice with a jolt that a guard-ghoul, one of the Master's most dangerous soldiers, is standing in front of you. It's entirely still, watching you closely. But you don't try to hide from its dreadful, piercing eyes – instead, you stay calm and trust in the power of a floppy hat and a shabby coat to see you through.

You're just an ordinary goblin hurrying to fetch water from the river. For a long moment, you feel as though the creature is about to step into your path and confront you, but to your relief it doesn't move and you walk past it unchallenged.

"Thanks, friendly farmer," you whisper to yourself. As soon as you're on the dock, you scamper to the end and untie a rowing boat. Apologising to the shadows for stealing it, you hop in and slip out onto the dark water. No one sees you go.

Turn to **178**.

175

Your weapon spins end over end and thumps into the bat rider's breastplate. The blow knocks him out of his saddle, and as you dive out of the way you hear a scream which fades into nothingness. The rider has tumbled over the cliff with your weapon still lodged in his armour. The bat streaks down the cliff in pursuit but it can't catch up. Instead, you watch it hover over the broken body on the rocks far below, shrieking in despair and rage. You turn away and hurry towards the waystone, glancing up nervously at the sky.

Delete the WEAPON you used from your LOG BOOK and turn to **257**.

176

You walk into the dim, hushed wood. The sky disappears, blocked out by the branches that twist overhead and the thick canopy of new spring leaves. There's no sun in the wood, only a cool green light, and it smells of mushrooms and rot. The narrow road that you're following runs straight as an arrow beneath the silent trees. So much moss is growing between the cobbles that it feels as if you're walking on a thick carpet, but the strangest thing is how tidy it is – someone, or something, must have swept all the fallen leaves and branches off the path.

At last, you come to a fork in the road. "Which way to Crow Cave?" you wonder out loud.

"THIS WAY," rumbles a deep voice. You look around. The forest is still and silent, and you see no one – but the voice seemed to come from the path to your right.

To follow the voice and take the right-hand path, turn to **264**.

If you want to go left instead, turn to **97**.

177

You climb over the giant tree trunk as carefully as you can, but your foot slips on a patch of moss and your fingers touch the rot. You snatch them away, but not before its poison has seeped into your skin. Your hand begins to blister and sting as you curse and hurry on down the path.

Deduct 1 LIFE point and turn to **194**.

178

The little boat glides swiftly down the river. The current is fast, so you don't have much rowing to do except to take an occasional stroke to steer. For a long time you half-expect Darkmoon to fly in and fry you off the water, but eventually you relax a little. It's the first time you've sat down in a long while and you suddenly feel just how tired you are. Your legs ache. For a while you just let yourself go, not thinking, watching the dark water slip past and listening to the soft whisper of the ripples against the boat. But soon enough your worries bubble to the surface. How are you going to get to Crow Cave? How close is the hunt behind you? Why did you steal the ring?

"Losing hope, mate?"

"Boggo!" you say as his face pops up out of the water beside you.

"Listen! I ain't got much energy left, so I'm going to keep it quick," he says. *"I grew up on this river, so I know where it'll take you. If you're aiming for Crow Cave, your best bet is to take the boat as far as Rocklaw Bridge. There's a bend in the river that takes you close to the caves."*

"Thanks!" you say.

"Don't thank me yet," he scowls. *"The problem is what you do next. See, the path after that either takes you through Phantom Forest or Battle Marsh. Neither's very pleasant."*

"Which way would you go?" you ask.

"My advice to you," he says, his voice starting to get quieter as he fades away, *"is that you should definitely NOT take the route that..."*

And then he's gone. You stare at the water and ponder. At least you have some kind of plan now, but it's hard to make a decision while you're so tired. Perhaps you should have a rest – you could pull the boat up under a tree and get some sleep. Tomorrow's going to be a long day...

If you want to take the time to rest, turn to **221**.

If you want to continue down the river, turn to **18**.

179

The cat's claws rake across your back as you're dashing for the exit. Trying to ignore the stinging pain, you shove it away and slam the door behind you.

Deduct 1 LIFE point and turn to **85**.

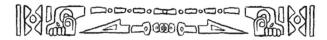

180

As you climb out of the parade ground and approach the bridge you hear a strange sound, as though someone is taking thousands of glasses and smashing them together: two rivers of lava are crashing into each other, and as they meet they crackle and splinter in the intense heat. You can see the forge looming on its island up ahead, shrouded in drifting smoke. The bridge is very open and you're going to be easy to spot when you cross it, so you stop for a moment, peering at what's on the other side. You can see several large figures sitting on the ground.

"Lick a crab! Are those griefers?" exclaims Boggo.

You've never seen a griefer before, but you know he's right because you've heard the stories - there's no mistaking their shaggy, hyena-like heads, or their giant axes, or their high-pitched giggling. Even Darkmoon doesn't employ griefers in his armies – they're far too wild and dangerous. But now you're going to have to get past a pack of them.

To try and sneak across the bridge, turn to **301**.

To try and climb along the underside of the bridge to avoid being spotted, turn to **325**.

If you have a vial of LAUGHING SYRUP, turn to **284**.

You pull out the ring and slip it on your finger, but nothing happens.

"YOU THINK YOU CAN USE THAT WRETCHED THING AGAINST ME?" growls the dragon. "I WILL NOT LET IT HAPPEN AGAIN IN MY FOREST."

It chuckles so loudly that all the trees around you shake, then it suddenly bends down and bites off your head, spitting it out high over the treetops.

182

You set off across the swamp, but almost immediately realise that leaving the path was a very bad idea – within a few steps the mud starts sucking you down, until with a sickening squelch your legs start to disappear into it. Grabbing hold of a fern, you pull yourself out – but not before you've sliced your leg on a sharp rock. Safely back on the path, you take another look at the suit of armour – somehow you're going to have to find your way past it.

Deduct 1 LIFE point and turn to **220**.

183

You sneak up the broken stairs and creep across the upper floor. The wall looks very fragile and a huge stone block is teetering on the edge, directly above the floating orb. You give it a hefty shove. The block tips over and drops straight onto the creature, which pops with a satisfying splat. Acid jelly and half-digested skeletons explode across the street.

Gain 1 ABILITY point and turn to **352**.

184

The smallest of the lizardfolk glances quickly at the hobtoads, but the guards are clearly not laughing. She snorts with derision. "Never speak to one of your betters again, goblin!" she snaps and slaps you hard across the cheek, raking you with her nails.

Deduct 1 LIFE point.

If you haven't talked to the minotaur and want to, turn to **37**.

If you want to look for another way out, turn to **327**.

185

The guard-ghoul looks into your eyes and for a moment you think it can't see you... then it breaks into a hideous grin and shrieks with triumph. It calls to its oarsmen to stop and points directly at your hiding place. There's only one way to survive this... the ring. As soon as you think of it, the ring has somehow slipped onto your finger and everything you see is surrounded by pale fire again. What you do next doesn't seem to come from you, but from the ring itself.

"SINK THEM!" you shout. At once, dozens of ghostly hands rise from the river and flip the boat upside down. The ghoul and the goblin rowers splash into the water, but before they can even shout in alarm they are dragged below. Soon there's nothing to see but the ripples.

You rip the ring off your finger, breathing hard. Those were goblins that you've just drowned – ordinary goblins like you and Boggo. They were only following orders, they had no evil in their hearts, and you killed them. You look down at the ring in your palm, wanting more than ever to be rid of it, to be rid of what it makes you do and then you wonder if Darkmoon knows what you've just done.

Fill in the next section of the RING TRACKER on your LOG BOOK. Then roll one dice.

If the number is equal to or lower than your RING SCORE, turn to **167**.

If the total is higher than your RING SCORE, turn to **273**.

186

You grit your teeth and ignore the furnace heat. Every breath is a struggle as the boiling vapours scorch your lungs, but you continue to inch your way along out of sight. The swirling smoke helps to conceal you as you get nearer and nearer to the opposite bank. When you're nearly there, a fight breaks out among the griefers and you seize your chance. As they thump and curse each other and roll around on the floor, you hop down from the bridge and creep past in the smoke.

Turn to **64**.

187

You're halfway across the kitchen with your basket when a huge hand grabs you by the shoulder and spins you round.

"Ah Groucho," you say, staring up at the head chef. "How nice to..."

"GOBLIN, GET THESE INGREDIENTS FROM THE SPICE PANTRY!" roars Groucho. He's got a huge cleaver in his hand, but he puts it down to shove a long list of ingredients in your face. "BE QUICK, OR I'LL COOK YOU IN MY SURPRISE PIE!"

You hurry over to the spice pantry, which is packed from floor to ceiling with all the most exotic and expensive ingredients in the land. It smells incredible, but you don't have time to stand around enjoying the aroma. You stare at the list in your hand, and gaze back up at the shelves.

Look at the list below, and the picture on the next page. You need to find all seven ingredients Groucho has chosen to cook in his famous Surprise Pie. Each of the ingredients has a shelf-number. To find the answer, add all seven shelf-numbers together and turn to that entry.

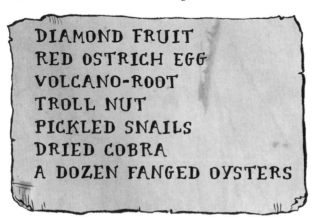

DIAMOND FRUIT
RED OSTRICH EGG
VOLCANO-ROOT
TROLL NUT
PICKLED SNAILS
DRIED COBRA
A DOZEN FANGED OYSTERS

If you can't work it out, turn to **308**.

As you walk deeper into the forest, a sudden bird call makes you look up, and you see a magpie flying overhead. You get the eerie feeling that it's been staring down among the trees, looking for you. Calling again, the magpie turns and swoops towards you. It all happens so fast that you don't have time to draw your weapon before it is upon you. Its sharp claws rake across your face, and then it flaps away, cawing in triumph.

Deduct 1 LIFE point and turn to **194**.

189

As you press the third button, a different painting on the wall swivels outwards to reveal a spiral staircase winding down beyond it. Gain 1 ABILITY point.

"Thanks Boggo!" you say, turning to him to celebrate... but the ghost has vanished. You step into the secret staircase, tugging the picture frame tightly back into place behind you until it clicks shut. It's very dark and the stone slabs are thick with dust – but the space between the walls is surprisingly roomy. Here and there, chinks in the wall send arrows of light through the gloom. You spiral down into the dimness, hearing the uproar in the castle around you – shouts and bangs echo softly through the stones. You shiver when you realise that you must be the cause of all that mayhem. Lost in these thoughts, you come to an abrupt stop when you realise you're face to face with a dragon! In the light of a small window, you can see its outstretched wings and gaping jaws... then you realise they're made of stone. It's just a statue. You chuckle nervously and start to step past it, but as you do so you hear a loud click...

Roll one dice then add your SNEAK level and WITS level to it.

If your total is 6 or higher, turn to **124**.

If your total is 5 or lower, turn to **230**.

190

Sliding into the dimly lit tent, you find big heaps of clothes that smell of old wool and damp. You slip through the narrow aisles between them, searching for something goblin-sized to wear. The only thing you find that's the right size is a jester's outfit in a vibrant green-and-yellow check... you're not exactly going to blend into the crowd wearing that. There's also a golden tunic with a hood, but it's a bit too big for you. Which one will draw less attention?

Boggo's face pops out of the heap of clothes, grinning mischievously. "*I reckon the jester costume is made for you,*" he chortles. "*You know some jokes, right? Here's one: Why is it a bad idea to play cards with big cats?*"

He waggles his ears, and you sigh. "I don't know, Boggo," you mutter, "and we don't really have time to–"

"*Because they're all cheetahs!*" he interrupts, squeaking with laughter at his own joke. You put your finger to your lips, then hold up the two outfits, trying to decide...

To choose the jester's outfit, turn to **122**.

To choose the golden tunic, turn to **292**.

The spider's black jaws sink into your hand. The bite stings and numbs at the same time, making you feel sleepy, but before it can attack again you kick out and send it spinning across the room. Luckily, it then retreats into its web, but your hand is swelling up like a balloon.

Cursing your luck, and with a painful throbbing in your thumb, you carry on down the stairs.

Deduct 1 SNEAK point and turn to **285**.

192

The goblin's body is still warm. You prise his fingers open and a wooden whistle tumbles loose. It looks just like the whistle on the strange sign that you saw, but as you reach out to pick it up, you hear loud rustling and whirl around to find a giant plant lunging towards you, its mouth open wide. Dozens of glistening, pointy teeth are closing in on your head.

To run to the other end of the balcony, turn to **109**.

To carry on trying to grab the whistle, turn to **280**.

193

After staring at the armour pacing up and down for a while and memorising its routine, you think you know exactly the moment to sneak past it. Darting forward, you've almost made it... when it turns unexpectedly and strides straight towards you. Trapped against the wall of the trench and trying to scrabble out, you feel its fist slam into your back.

Deduct 1 LIFE point.

To try and run away, turn to **169**.

To stand and fight the armour, turn to **35**.

194

Wearying, you trudge on through the forest. It can't be too far to Crow Cave now and you're just thinking that maybe you might make it out of here alive when you hear a terrifying roar. A strange bear-like creature is crashing through the trees towards you. Its body is covered in black rot and its eyes are wide and ferocious. As your hand goes to your weapon, you remember the tree dragon's warning: "DO NOT HARM MY CREATURES OR MY FOREST." But surely this grisly beast can't be one of the tree dragon's creatures?

To run away, turn to **100**.

To stand your ground and fight, turn to **291**.

195

Night is falling, and glowing sparks are rising into the sky above the village. You hurry down the line of shacks and turn into a wider road that leads to the jetty. It's ablaze with light and full of hurry and scurry: several houses are burning at the other end and goblins have formed a bucket-line to put out the flames. It's not difficult to pass unnoticed through the mayhem. Grabbing a bucket, you run for the jetty where you can see a number of rowing boats tied up.

If you have a DISGUISE, turn to **174**.

If you don't, turn to **56**.

196

You climb the shattered stairs to the upper floor and spot an escape route up and over the roofs. But as you run across, you fail to spot a broken floorboard. It shatters under your weight and throws you over the edge into the street below. You land with a sickening crash right in front of the waiting orb.

Deduct 1 LIFE point and turn to **27**.

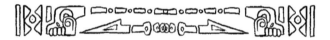

197

You've never spent much time in the woods, but you know just enough about them to spot needlegrass – and there's a large patch of it right in front of you. With a smile, you remember your grandpa's warning: "Purple roots will slice your boots!" Once you've edged around the razor-sharp stems, you feel rather pleased with yourself and stride on towards Blackwell.

Turn to **147**.

198

Thinking of the old farmer's warning, you crouch on your heels under a dense, low-hanging bush, hiding until you are sure the magpie has definitely flown on. You take a moment to think – you've been running for so long now that it's hard to believe you had a normal life just yesterday. If you can call working in Darkmoon's tower normal. As you're lost in these thoughts, you spot something glinting, half-buried in the earth by the side of the road. You scratch away the mud to reveal a small glass vial with the words LAUGHING SYRUP scribbled on its faded label.

Add the LAUGHING SYRUP to your LOG BOOK and turn to **194**.

199

With a sigh of surprise, the guard-ghoul falls to the ground, dead. You quickly search its pockets, and find a compass, which you tuck into your waistcoat next to the ring.

"*I thought you were a goner, for sure,*" says Boggo. "*Now it really is time to leave.*"

You stare around the room again. Should you take the risk of carrying on down the stairs or is it better to sneak out of the window?

Add the COMPASS to your LOG BOOK.

To take the stairs, turn to **62**.

To climb out of the window, turn to **168**.

You decide to follow Boggo's plan and follow the trails. Sadly, just as you feared, they lead you straight to the nest of the giant snails. Worse, in the slimy, egg-filled corridor up ahead, two of the snails are fighting, or perhaps talking, it's difficult to be sure – but as you draw back into the shadows, you kick a pebble and it rattles across the stone floor. The sound instantly brings the blind monsters surging towards you. In desperation you pluck an item from your pack and hurl it back down the passage you came from, hoping it will distract them and draw them away. To your intense relief, it does...

Creeping on beyond the slime-encrusted nest, you begin to hear a distant murmur, like the roaring of a great fire. You follow the noise and the air begins to grow warmer. Suddenly you emerge into a vast, smoky space. Below you a precipice drops away to an enormous underground city, glowing red from the flames of the lava rivers that surge through it.

Choose one item or weapon and delete it from your LOG BOOK, then turn to **307**.

201

The goblin ghost screams terrible insults and disgusting oaths as you walk away. It makes you glad you didn't help it. Up ahead, the mist parts for a moment. You catch a glimpse of a ruined castle on a hill in the distance, and your pulse quickens. Crow Cave...

Turn to **250**.

202

You're so tired, so worn out by all you've given to reach this moment that when it finally comes you don't have the strength you need. Darkmoon holds you at bay with a series of defensive spells, then suddenly blasts pale fire from his outstretched palms. Iron Mane is ripped in half, and your broken body thuds to the ground. The Master strolls over and takes the ring from your helpless fingers as you gasp your last few breaths. As he slips it on, he stares into your eyes and grins in terrible triumph. It's the last thing you ever see.

203

You feel the stinking breath of the plant on your neck as its great jaws slam shut behind you. After risking so much to snatch the whistle, you immediately put it to your lips and blow. The note it produces is low and pure, and the heads of all the plants immediately droop as if they're asleep. Deciding it's high time to get off this balcony, you look around you for a way out.

Gain 1 ABILITY point, and add the WOODEN WHISTLE to your LOG BOOK, then turn to **4**.

204

The fog remains thick and damp, swirling around your face, and as you trudge on it's hard to keep track of time. Big white bones poke out of the ground here and there – you can't imagine how many died in the battle or how savage a fight it must have been. You find yourself wishing Boggo would turn up to tell you a silly joke, but there's no sign of him. After a long trudge you come to a fork in the path. By now you've lost all sense of direction and have no idea which way will take you towards Crow Cave.

If you have a COMPASS, turn to **46**.

If you don't, turn to **322**.

205

You're scrabbling about for a weapon when your hand falls on the bottle of hot sauce that you've had in your pouch for so long. Skipping backwards, you unscrew the lid and hurl the jar. It sinks deep into the orb's flesh and the hole immediately starts smoking – you can see thin tendrils of spicy sauce snaking through the jelly, which has stopped moving forward and is now hanging in place, quivering.

"What did your mum call that sauce again?" you mutter to Boggo as the orb begins to shrivel into a wet smoking puddle.

"*Mum calls it MAGMA!*" says Boggo. "*It's best to only eat a little bit.*"

Making a mental note never to try any of the sauce, you hurry away.

Gain 1 ABILITY point and turn to **352**.

206

Marcox steps towards you and you instantly know that he has seen right through you.

"Give it to me," he hisses.

You watch in horror as your hand reaches into your pocket and pulls out the ring. You place it in his outstretched palm, powerless to resist.

"And now – you DIE!" hisses Marcox.

The world turns black.

207

Suddenly the dragon's eyes snap open and she sniffs the air with its giant nostrils.

"BY THE GODS!" she breathes. "HAVE YOU BROUGHT IT?"

"Brought?" you stammer. "Brought what?" The dragon lifts her head and the rocks and rubble cascade down around it, smashing on the ground.

"MY EGG, FOOLISH GOBLIN! DO YOU HAVE IT?"

For a moment you don't know what she's talking about. Then you remember – it seems like an age has passed since you pulled the egg from the basin in Darkmoon's tower. You reach inside your shirt and hold it out, your fingers trembling slightly. The dragon doesn't speak, but takes the egg gently from your hands with her teeth. Her breath is furnace-hot, and a single tear rolls down her cheek.

"IT HAS BEEN SO LONG," she whispers. "I DID NOT THINK THIS DAY WOULD COME." She places the egg carefully down beside her, as if it was the most important thing in the world. "MY EGG WAS STOLEN FROM ME. IT IS MY LAST EGG, AND THE LAST HOPE OF MY KIND. I WAS TOLD IF I WAITED HERE IT WOULD BE BROUGHT TO ME. BUT I'VE WAITED SO LONG THAT I DOUBTED THE OLD LADY'S PROPHECY... AND YET STILL YOU CAME." She stares at you, looking solemn.

"YOU ARE AN INSIGNIFICANT CREATURE, GOBLIN, BUT YOU HAVE DONE ME THE GREATEST SERVICE. I WILL BE FOREVER IN YOUR DEBT. TAKE THIS AS AN OATH THAT WHEN YOU NEED ME MOST, I WILL COME." She pulls a scale from her shoulder with her teeth and lays it in front of you.

"NOW GO," she says, turning back to her egg. "I HAVE WASTED TOO MUCH TIME ALREADY."

Add the DRAGON SCALE to your LOG BOOK and turn to **218**.

208

The fog is wet and cold and soaks into your clothes and under your skin. You walk for several hours but the sun never pierces the gloom. At first you see no traces of the battle that once took place here – all you notice are lots of little rocks. You kick one as you walk along, and it crumbles into dust... with a jolt, you realise that the "rocks" are actually bones. The marsh feels very different after that, and you tread carefully around the bones. Sometimes the mist curls in such a way that you think you see silhouettes of people or goblins or minotaurs, but when you look again there's nothing but the dripping, white cold all around you.

It's almost completely silent... or is it? Somewhere in the distance, you start to hear a strange clanking noise. It grows steadily louder, a rhythmic plod as if something heavy and rusty is stomping back and forth – and the path seems to be taking you closer and closer to it. The fog is so thick that you're only a few metres away when you see it: a suit of rusting armour, marching back and forth over and over again across the same patch of land. It's been marching so long that it's worn a deep trench in the wet earth. You're going to have to get past it somehow, but to either side the marsh looks dangerously swampy.

If you want to leave the path to avoid the armour and try your luck in the swamp, turn to **182**.

To walk along the path, straight past the armour, turn to **220**.

209

The sapling trots jauntily beside you – it's a bizarre creature, all spindly wooden knees and elbows, but it cheers you up to have a companion as you walk through the murky forest. You cross a little stream and the sapling stops to munch on a patch of blueberry bushes growing by the water. Feeling hungry, you follow its lead and eat until you're full.

Add 2 LIFE points.

After a while, the forest begins to change. The trees to the right of the path are covered in the same black, mushroomy rot that you removed from the sapling's hoof, and many of them seem to be dead. There's no rot on the cobbled road itself or in the forest on the other side, so it seems as if the road is a barrier that stops the rot from spreading.

The sapling is trotting along towards an old oak tree when it suddenly whimpers and clambers up into its branches. A moment later you discover why – with a bloodcurdling howl, a big dark shape comes smashing through the trees towards you. The sapling whinnies from its high perch, calling to you perhaps. You could probably climb up to join it there, but maybe it would be better to stand your ground and fight?

To stay where you are and fight the monster, turn to **291**.

To climb the tree, turn to **214**.

210

You find Stinker's skull exactly where he described it, and once you've prised it out of the sucking mud he shouts instructions, sounding increasingly excited, to guide you safely back to where you started.

"*At last!*" he says. "*Drop the skull in the water now.*"

"Hey – what about the magic sword?" you say. "That was the bargain, Stinker."

"*I can't leave the puddle until I've got my head back, can I?*" he squeaks. "*Just drop it!*"

You do as he says, watching the skull splash under the surface, and he cackles with glee.

"*My head! My beautiful head! I can leave at last!*" he exclaims, his voice already starting to fade. "*So long, sucker! You're quite a fool for a goblin.*"

"Wait, what?" you shout. "No! We had a deal."

"*Where I'm going you can't follow, unless you're dead of course,*" he says, drifting away. "*So actually I have a feeling I may see you sooooooon....*"

With that, the ghost is gone and silence settles over Battle Marsh once more. You kick the puddle in disgust, but there's nothing there now. You can't believe you've been betrayed by a fellow goblin. Snorting in disgust, you trudge on towards Crow Cave.

Turn to **55**.

211

You run on, but your lungs are burning and your legs feel weak. The armour is never going to slow down, never going to stop. The soft ground saps your strength, making every step a little harder than the last. Up ahead you spot a strange, bright green pond just off the path. No grass or plants are growing around it, and emerald steam is rising from its surface. It looks dangerous: you get the feeling that if anything goes in there, it probably won't come out.

Knowing this is your only chance, you leave the path and squelch your way towards the pond's edge, dragging your feet free from the sucking mud with every step. The pondwater smells even worse than it looks, a metallic reek that burns your nostrils. The unstoppable armour has followed you of course and is sloshing closer and closer until it's right behind you, reaching out to grab you with its metal fingers. You wait till the very last second then try to jump across the narrowest part of the pond.

Roll one dice and add it to your STRENGTH level.

If your total is 5 or higher, turn to **224**.

If your total is 4 or lower, turn to **93**.

You have enough problems right now – the last thing you need is an imaginary ghost. Deciding that it's just your panicked mind that's making you see things, you hurry on down the stairs. No one seems to be about and you start to think you might make it to the bottom unseen, but then you hear raised voices coming from far below. Suddenly Boggo's head emerges through the floor right in front of you.

"*You always thought you knew better,*" he huffs, floating higher. "*Don't know why I'm even bothering, but listen.*" He tries to jab you in your chest, but his finger goes straight through. "*They're shutting everyone who comes down these stairs into a room and holding them there. Now, there's a roof garden through this window – you could climb out onto it?*"

You close your eyes and try to banish this imaginary Boggo, but when you open them again he's very much still there, pointing at the window. It's hard to believe, but it seems that Boggo's ghost is trying to help you.

"*Yes, yes. I'm still here, and you can see me,*" he says. "*It's something to do with that cursed ring you stole. Which was a great idea, by the way! What do you plan to do with it?*"

"I'm not sure..." you mutter, glancing nervously down as the sound of voices gets closer.

"*Well, I'd bet my gold tooth that the rebels in that cave we've just heard about would be mighty interested in having that ring. It's powerful magic and it might help them. You could warn them that Darkmoon is coming for them too. Then they might not end up like me...*"

As reluctant as you are to take advice from someone who's just been killed, you have to admit that this sounds like the best plan you've got.

"*Right, so you need to get out of this tower,*" he says, pointing at the window again and speaking more quickly as the stamp of many feet comes echoing up the stairs, only a few seconds away now. You nod, and climb out.

Turn to **287**.

213

The sun is sinking as you climb through the patchy rain. The wind whips clouds across the sky, giving you brief sunset glimpses of the fields and farms below. Staring into the distance, you feel every hair on the back of your neck stand up – far away you can see a snaking line of smoke, dotted by thousands of fiery pinpricks. The smoke is rising all along the New Road, which means Boggo was right: the Master's army is heading for Crow Cave. Now that you're listening for the sound, you can hear the dim throbbing of their drums. Even worse, you spot the swooping shapes of bat-riders heading in different directions. Several seem to be veering off towards the hills where you're standing.

You walk faster and try to keep off the top of the ridge, out of sight. After a steady climb, you come to a well-trodden track and you spot a soggy little crowd of travellers camped by the side of it. They are humans – a family by the looks of it – and they haven't seen you yet. Part of you knows it would be wisest to sneak past them, because a goblin is unlikely to get a friendly greeting from any human.

On the other hand, you're not sure exactly where Crow Cave is, and maybe they could help you.

To try to sneak around the human family, turn to **354**.

To try to talk to them, turn to **3**.

214

You climb the tree, only just in time, as the slavering beast bursts onto the road and shrieks in frustration, never taking its eyes off you. It looks as though it was once was a bear, but it's hard to be sure because now it's all black rot and hollow bones. It smashes into the trunk of your tree so hard that the branch you're clinging to shudders. The sapling whimpers softly and climbs higher. You're about to follow when, below, you see a sudden, silent tangle of limbs and bark. Some giant creature has melted out of the forest below and pinned the bear to the ground. It looks like a dragon but it's made of roots and twigs, and now this tree dragon is weaving a magical basket of branches around the rotten bear's body before it can move.

"THANK YOU FOR CARING FOR MY SAPLING," it booms, calmly looking up at you as the bear struggles and roars. Then with a grunt of effort the dragon squeezes the cage tight around the rotten bear, killing it instantly. To your surprise, it then bows its head and kneels over the corpse. The little sapling hops down from the tree and climbs onto its shoulder.

"COME GOBLIN," says the dragon. "LET US REMEMBER THIS POOR CREATURE AND LET US HOPE IT IS AT PEACE NOW."

You climb down a little hesitantly and kneel by the body, watching in amazement as flowers of every colour spring up from the woven branches of the cage and cover it up. Soon all that remains of the bear is a hummock by the side of the road, thickly carpeted in spring blooms.

"FOLLOW ME PLEASE," booms the dragon, and you decide not to argue.

Gain 1 ABILITY point and turn to **146**.

215

You open an iron gate, climb a short staircase and emerge into the daylight, quickly glancing around at the fields either side of the road ahead... all empty for now. You're amazed to have escaped Darkmoon's tower, although there's no time to dwell on your success. Normally, Crow Cave would be a two-day journey by the New Road from here – but you know your journey will be far from normal. You glance back up at the black bulk of the tower – bats are spiralling out from the tallest spire, each one with a tiny rider clinging to its back. You know exactly who the bat-riders are looking for, and there's not much cover out here in the fields. Looking ahead, there's a little wood that fringes the track. You'd be less obvious under the trees, but your journey would be slower too.

To continue down the track, turn to **255**.

To take cover in the trees, turn to **43**.

You step slowly backwards away from the wolf, staring into its yellow eyes. You know you can't outrun it, and you don't know what else to do.

"Don't worry," you say. "I'm your friend. I don't have an–"

Without warning, the wolf darts forward and sinks its teeth into your leg. You leap away, but not before it's opened up a gash in your thigh. It circles you with its teeth bared, then crouches low, getting ready to spring... when a huge tree branch swings out of the shadows and scoops it up into the air. The wolf whines with confusion and surprise, but it's powerless to resist.

"WELL DONE, YOUNG GOBLIN," booms the tree dragon, leaning down to look you in the eye. "THOSE WHO HARM THE FOREST HARM ONLY THEMSELVES. NOW LET'S SEE IF WE CAN FIND FRIEND WOLF SOMETHING BETTER TO EAT."

The dragon rustles away, slipping quickly back into the forest with the wolf still cradled in its claws.

Deduct 1 LIFE point and gain 1 ABILITY point, then turn to **48**.

The orb is relentless. You try to keep it at arm's length, but it takes no notice of your weapon and pushes you to the ground. It starts to settle over you like a soft, devouring pillow until it comes into contact with the ring in your pocket. With a disgusted shudder, it spits you out and squelches away at great speed. You've survived, but the orb's acid has left its mark on you.

Lose 1 STRENGTH, 1 SNEAK and 1 WITS point, and turn to **352**.

218

You're now walking near a steep-sided lava canal which flows slow and thick as treacle. There's a black crust on the surface, which belches and bubbles with red-hot spurts of fire. Smoke from the lava swirls around you, making it hard to see ahead. But when it clears for a moment you find yourself arriving at another big square – with a sunken parade ground in the centre. It's full of iron statues – humans, goblins, minotaurs, lizardfolk... dozens and dozens of them standing in neat rows like soldiers on a parade ground. They're all wearing the same old-fashioned armour, and through a series of archways you glimpse hundreds more of them in a vast room beyond.

You're getting close to your goal now: at the end of this plaza rises the bridge that leads to the looming shape of the forge itself.

"*Nearly there*," rumbles the voice of the Iron Smith in your head. "*Tell me, ringbearer, do you think you could lead this army of mine? Do you see that platform over there?*" Your gaze falls on a raised section at the centre of the square with a few larger statues standing on top of it. "*Those are my generals*," says the Smith. "*I wonder if you can tell me which one was my favourite?*"

You arrive at the platform and examine the statues. There's no reason to pick one over another.

"*I shall give you three clues, young goblin*," booms the Smith. "*My favourite was known as the Young General. They relied on their wits, not a bladed weapon. And they feared no ambush because they kept their ears uncovered.*"

Look at the picture on the next page. If you can work out which general was the Iron Smith's favourite, add up the numbers of all the other statues and turn to that number.

If you can't work it out, turn to **346**.

You walk up the hill slowly with your hands in the air, trying to show that you're friendly. "I'm on the run from Darkmoon!" you shout. "I've stolen something. It's–"

Suddenly a knife appears at your throat, and whiskers tickle your ear. Squirming around, you find yourself in the grip of an enormous cat. "One more step, goblin, and I gut you like a fish," she purrs.

A huge human guard covered in tattoos steps out of the shadows and begins strolling towards you with a casual grin. "Ask the goblin what it's stolen, Anna," he says.

"You heard the man – what've you stolen, goblin?" whispers the cat in your ear. The edge of her knife shivers against your skin.

"I took the Night Ring," you say.

"You what?" says the tattooed guard, his smile swiftly fading.

"The PROPHECY!" hisses the cat. "Can it actually be true?" You realise that in her shock she's let you go, and you step away, glad to be free of her claws. You reach into your pocket and pull out the ring.

"Y-you... you're the RINGBEARER!" stutters the guard as he sinks to his knees and raises his arms in the air. "LADS! LADS! THE PROPHECY IS TRUE! THE RINGBEARER'S HERE!"

Turn to **95**.

You creep closer to the clanking suit of armour. Its visor is rusted shut so you have no idea if someone or something is still inside it. The trench it's gouged in the swamp with its marching is very deep, so it's going to be a challenge to sneak past it.

Roll one dice and add it to your SNEAK level.

If your total is 7 or higher, turn to page **347**.

If your total is 6 or lower, turn to page **193**.

221

You find a willow tree leaning out over the stream and tie the boat up beneath its long, drooping branches. It's like a tent – and in the dark your little boat should be well hidden here. You curl up and close your eyes. Rocking gently on the current, you drift off to sleep.

Add 3 LIFE points.

You wake up with a start a few hours later – you can hear drumming in the distance. It grows louder and louder, and then a long, narrow boat sweeps into view. Lit by flaming torches, a dozen goblin oarsmen are churning the water white. A guard-ghoul stands at the back, steering the boat and scanning the river. You duck down low.

If you have a BLANKET, turn to **262**.

If you don't, turn to **108**.

The vast kitchen is one of the largest rooms in the tower. It's full of spicy smoke and steam, shouts and smells and swearing. Most of the swearing comes from the enormous head chef, who is lumbering across the room waving a giant frying pan.

"*You've done well pal, getting here,*" says a voice in your ear. "*Didn't think you'd make it.*"

"Boggo!" you whisper. You're delighted to see the ghost again. "Where did you go?"

"*Took a breather. It's awful tiring, being dead. Anyhow, you got an escape plan yet?*"

You don't have a plan – but you'll need one fast, so you scan the busy room, looking for a friendly face. Goblins are working everywhere, washing, slicing, peeling, sweeping, and carrying baskets, crates and plates. You finally spot your friend Midge: she's chopping her way through a big bag of onions. Maybe she knows a way out? Nearby, left alone on a countertop, you also notice an unwatched plate of deep-fried spice-beetle. The smell is enough to make your stomach rumble and you suddenly realise how hungry you are.

To talk to Midge, turn to **28**.

To pinch some crispy beetle, turn to **331**.

223

The soldier spots you as you step forward and immediately drops the girl to focus on you.

"Got a problem, goblin?" he snarls and draws his sword. You have no choice but to fight him – but at least the child is safe. As you circle each other, you're both surprised when the girl jumps high on the soldier's back and tries to blind him by wrapping her scarf around his head. Seizing your chance, you dart in to attack.

Add 1 to your first attack roll in this fight, because the girl is on the soldier's back and is distracting him. If your attack is successful, keep adding 1 to your attack rolls until you miss – then you lose your advantage as the soldier throws the girl off his back and can fight freely.

HUMAN SOLDIER

Rounds: 5   Damage: 2

YOU

If you win, turn to **144**.

If you lose, turn to **343**.

224

You jump high and land with a soft squelch on the other side of the pond. The relentless suit of armour doesn't jump after you but plods straight into the bright green water. Its legs start to melt at once, and within seconds it's chest-deep and sinking fast. White smoke fills the air as the metal burns, until all that remains is a single arm still reaching for you, then that too is gone. Breathing hard, you hurry away.

Gain 1 ABILITY point and turn to **204**.

You drag the unconscious hobtoad behind a curtain, grabbing her truncheon as you let go.

Add the TRUNCHEON to your LOG BOOK. You now have a weapon and no longer need to subtract 1 from all your rolls in a fight.

You set off quickly down the stairs, but soon you hear the sound of heavy boots approaching.

"Hurry up you fools!" It's the voice of Marcox, the Master's butler. Fear flows through you and stops you dead in your tracks. Marcox doesn't miss a single speck of dust on a polished floor – and he loves to flog goblins half to death if they haven't cleaned up properly. You can't imagine what he'd do to a goblin who'd stolen the Night Ring.

If you want to try to bluff your way past Marcox, turn to **135**.

If you want to squeeze into a shadowy corner and hope for the best, turn to **40**.

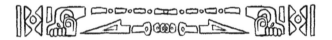

226

"OK," you say. "Let's do it."

"*You're a diamond!*" says Boggo. "*Follow me...*"

You creep towards the riverside, with Boggo floating just ahead of you. The soldiers are everywhere, barging around the village and kicking down doors. As you sneak round a corner you see a soldier dragging a goblin child out of her house by her hair. She's screaming and struggling to escape.

To try to creep past them, turn to **159**.

To try to help the girl, turn to **223**.

You pick a single berry and pop it in your mouth, half-expecting the tree dragon to jump out of the forest and squash you flat. But nothing happens. Maybe picking berries is permitted, or maybe the dragon isn't watching you right now. Pushing your luck, you pick some more and gulp them down, and your rumbling stomach is grateful.

Add 2 LIFE points and turn to **42**.

228

You carefully slip between the glimmering strands of web, while keeping a watchful eye on the darkness above you. Even for a goblin, it's a tight squeeze.

Roll one dice and add your SNEAK level and your WITS level.

If your total is 7 or higher, turn to **65**.

If your total is 6 or lower, turn to **342**.

229

You spot a sun-shaped symbol in the centre of the minotaur's breastplate and it stirs a memory. Reaching inside your shirt you draw out the MINOTAUR'S CHARM and as you hold it out you can see the same symbol on it. The minotaur takes a step back and lowers her scythe. *"How came you by that?"* she asks. As you explain, a look of amazement settles on her face. *"I never thought this day would come. You are our hope,"* she whispers. *"Go quickly, you must hasten to the end now. Fulfil your destiny and release us all! And remember – when the time comes, you must destroy the ring!"* She starts to fade away. *"May my blessing be your guide..."*

Make a note of GOLDENHEART'S BLESSING in your LOG BOOK. If you fail in a skill roll, you can reverse the outcome and succeed instead. After you've used the blessing once, cross it out.

Turn to **288**.

230

A wave of fire blasts from the dragon's mouth and curls around your leg as you leap for safety. You roll down a few steps to put the flames out, but your ankle is burned.

Deduct 1 LIFE point and turn to **111**.

You tell your story, trying to keep to just the important bits, and watch the dragon very closely. But her expression is unreadable. When you come to an uncertain finish she sits up, shaking off the timber and tiles from its back. The ground rumbles and it feels like a mountain is growing up beside you – you had no idea she was actually that big.

"YOU'RE A BRAVE LITTLE THING," she says. "AND I BELIEVE WE HAVE A COMMON ENEMY. THIS FOOL WIZARD THAT YOU STOLE FROM, HE STOLE SOMETHING IMPORTANT FROM ME, SOMETHING OF FAR GREATER WORTH THAN THE TRINKET YOU CARRY. I WILL HELP YOU IN YOUR FIGHT. TAKE THIS AS A TOKEN OF A MOTHER'S PROMISE. WHEN YOU FACE HIM, I WILL FLY TO YOUR AID."

The dragon reaches out with a long claw and pulls a single scale from her shoulder, dropping it at your feet with a metallic clatter. It's the size of a soup plate, blackened and dented on one side and brilliant crimson on the other. When you pick it up, you're surprised to find that it weighs almost nothing.

"GO!" she roars. "FINISH YOUR QUEST! AND IF THE SKIES DARKEN WITH YOUR FOES, LOOK FOR ME GOBLIN. I SHALL NOT LET YOU DOWN. BUT FIRST, I MUST EAT. CENTURIES WITHOUT DINNER LEAVE ME WITH QUITE AN APPETITE."

She takes off in a cloud of dust, flapping her mighty wings with sharp cracks that echo off the walls. Rising fast, she soars on the warm air until she disappears through a hole in the ceiling.

"Not every day you see that," says Boggo.

Add the DRAGON SCALE to your LOG BOOK and turn to **218**.

232

The weapon glows softly as you take it in your hand – it has the unmistakable tingle of magic about it. Make a note in your LOG BOOK that it's enchanted. While using that weapon, every time you roll a double during a fight you can add one extra to your attack roll – so if you roll two 4s, you get 9 rather than 8.

"*Oh no!*" hisses Boggo. "*You took too long – someone's coming!*"

Turn to **333**.

233

You hitch the rope around the rocks and pull it tight using a sailor's knot your grandma taught you to tie. It's now stretched right across the path at ankle height and the relentless suit of armour is almost here. You hurry off down the path and it follows... stepping straight into your trap. Its legs tangle in the rope and it crashes to the ground, losing one of its feet and trapping its arms in the mud. It's going to be a long time before it can follow you again – even so you scamper off into the mist before it has the chance.

Gain 1 ABILITY point and delete the ROPE from your LOG BOOK, then turn to **204**.

234

You stare and stare at the gravestone but you can't work out the puzzle. The longer you look, the more aware you are of the time you're wasting. A couple of times you think you hear wings in the air overhead, but when you look up there's nothing.

"*Don't worry, ringbearer,*" says Shuggy. "*Not everyone's a genius. Come back to me when you've defeated Darkmoon, eh? We all believe in you.*"

"I'm sorry," you say.

"*Don't think about it,*" says Shuggy.

Shaking your head in disappointment, you trudge away from the graveyard.

Deduct 1 WITS point and turn to **101**.

235

The edges of your vision go dark as the plant's poison takes hold, then you stumble and fall to your knees. Fortunately you're unconscious long before the plant begins to feast on you.

236

You roar as you brace your legs against the front of the cart and pull.

"*YOU MAGGOT-BRAIN!*" screams Boggo.

Roll one dice and add it to your STRENGTH level.

If your total is 8 or higher, turn to **254**.

If your total is 7 or lower, turn to **80**.

237

As the air from the bellows meets the fire inside the pyramid, the flame begins to change. It burns first red, then white and finally sharpens into an ice-blue jet of pure heat that singes the hair from your skin when you stand too close.

"It is done," says the Iron Smith with a deep sigh of satisfaction. "You and I will craft such wonders here! And as I promised, you have revealed the path to my tomb..." At the far end of the forge the walls are sliding back to reveal an enormous doorway cast from iron.

"Open that door, and I can fully awake again," says the Iron Smith.

Turn to **156**.

238

You hang from the edge of the balcony, take a deep breath... then drop. You have plenty of time, as you plummet, to think that maybe this was a bad idea.

Roll one dice and add your SNEAK and STRENGTH levels.

If your total is 8 or higher, turn to **23**.

If your total is 7 or lower, turn to **49**.

239

Before you're even halfway to the bat-riders, a streak of silver thunders past you as the dragon appears and swoops down to attack, blazing fire from her gaping jaws. She slams into the bat-riders and scatters them like sparrows and they plummet, flaming and broken, towards the ground.

"LOOK TO THE FIGHT DOWN BELOW, RINGBEARER!" roars the dragon, biting a bat in half. "I WILL CONTROL THE SKY, BUT YOU ARE NEEDED ON THE GROUND!"

Turn to **119**.

240

You explain that you've run away from the tower after Darkmoon killed your best friend. But the old farmer doesn't seem to believe you. He drives a hard bargain and insists on getting something valuable in exchange for his floppy hat and coat.

"The hat's been in my family for fifty years," he explains with a gap-toothed grin. "It was first worn by my great-great-grandfather!"

To do a deal with him, you'll have to give him something in return. If you want to do this, delete any item (except the NIGHT RING) from your LOG BOOK and add DISGUISE in its place. If you don't have an item, then the deal can't take place.

The farmer is pleased with his haggling and begins to whistle cheerfully as you trudge on down the track to Blackwell.

Turn to **147**.

241

You know your only chance is a fast attack, so as the minotaur advances you dart forward, feint once to the right arm, once to the stomach and then swipe a killing blow straight across its throat.

"*NO!*" moans the ghost, but her aura is fading already. "*Ringbearer, you must... release us...*"

"*Don't worry about her,*" says the Iron Smith's voice in your head. "*She'll be back again next time – though I thought you dealt with her rather neatly. So many ringbearers have failed here.*"

Gain 1 ABILITY point and turn to **288**.

The crowd is so silent that you could hear a sparrow sneeze.

"As you all know, we have but little time," says the old lady. "In just a few hours, we will all be fighting for our lives. But that battle, and our triumph or our failure, will not finally be decided by us alone. We can buy some time, but it is the ringbearer who has the power to save us."

Your head swims as you try to take all of this in. Everyone is watching you.

"I'm afraid you, my goblin friend, are our only hope," she continues. "Regrettably I can't explain why – although you must understand this one thing: the ring chose you." She gestures to the crowd, pointing out various well-armed, dangerous-looking figures. "The ring didn't choose one of our brave heroes, or stealthy spies, or wise wizards. It chose you, a goblin, to be its champion."

"*Smart decision, I'd say,*" chuckles Boggo, grinning. "*It's about time us goblins got our chance in the big show, eh?*" You want to tell him to be quiet, but you don't want to make everyone think you're crazy, talking to nobody, so you simply frown.

Now the old lady points to the other end of the cave, deeper into the mountain, where a huge door of solid rock is sliced into the cave side. "As many of you know, the reason we chose this particular place to hide is that the tomb of the Iron Smith who forged the ring lies down there. The ring will open the door to his city and let you in, ringbearer, but what trials lie beyond I cannot say, for my dreams do not show me – and only you will be able to enter."

"Wait," you say. "Only me? That seems like a bad idea. What about all these heroes and thieves and wizards?"

"Only you," echoes the lady. "All we can do is show you the way, and pray that in there you find the path to our salvation."

The crowd mutters excitedly and a few people cheer. Everyone is still staring at you. Some of the faces are smiling and full of hope but others are scowling and you can see that they still doubt you. A little girl perched on her father's shoulders catches your eye and gives you a big, wide grin. You decide to remember her face, not the frowning ones.

"So I just walk in... now?" you mutter.

"Now," she says. "It is late already. Darkmoon's army is almost here."

A chant begins among the crowd, at first from a few people only, but gradually from everyone:

"Ringbearer! Ringbearer! Ringbearer!"

Before you know what's happening you're being pushed, almost carried, across the cave towards the door.

Turn to **78**.

243

You don't stop walking. The hobtoads grin and exchange glances.

"This should be fun," one chortles. "Seems this little gobbo's got a death wish." They charge towards you and you quickly realise that you've made a terrible mistake. As the hobtoads' spears poke and stab, you tumble back down the corridor. A speartip grazes your shoulder as you spin away, and then another catches you in the arm. You're not a warrior and you don't stand a chance of surviving this fight, let alone winning it. Is this the end of your quest already? As if in answer to that question, the ring shivers in your pocket.

Deduct 3 LIFE points and turn to **289**.

244

"I can't do that," you say. "I'm afraid of the ring – and I don't want to use it. I want to give it away – but maybe the person I give it to will help you?"

"HMMMM…" booms the tree dragon. "YOU WILL FIND IT HARDER THAN YOU THINK TO GIVE IT UP. ALL THE SAME, I CANNOT BUT RESPECT YOUR HESITATION TO TOUCH EVIL."

"I'm sorry," you say.

"IT IS YOUR CHOICE," says the dragon. "WHY APOLOGISE? COME – I WILL LEAD YOU TO THE CAVES."

Turn to **50**.

245

Bracing your legs against the walls of the shaft, you climb down the rope. Just as you suspected, the shaft leads to the kitchen – as you drop lower you hear the usual banging and shouting as lunch is prepared. You smell it too – pickled cabbage has a very particular stink. At the bottom you squeeze around the little elevator box that carries the food and shove the hatch open.

Turn to **222**.

246

You remember the note that you found. As you creep around the edge of the lake, the roar of the waterfall grows louder. The foam and spray make it easy to remain hidden, although the rocks are slippery. At first you're worried that the clue was wrong because there doesn't seem to be a path to follow, but when you're almost underneath the waterfall you spot a few worn steps carved so cunningly into the rock that they're only visible when you're right on top of them. You climb carefully behind the curtain of tumbling water, getting soaked by spray, and find a thin passage cut into the mountain ahead of you. Squeezing inside it, you emerge after a few moments into a tunnel lit by glowing green moss on its ceiling. All along the walls, there are faded paintings that seem to show a bearded man brandishing a huge hammer.

Gain 1 ABILITY point.

Gradually the roar of the waterfall fades and you begin to hear voices ahead... the rebels! The smell of cooking meat is mixed with the stench of garbage, and you wonder how long they've been hiding in here like rats. As you draw closer to the sounds, the tunnel shrinks again until you have to squeeze through it sideways. Finally, you find yourself on the rim of a large bowl-shaped cave lit by huge clumps of the green glowmoss high above. The front part of the cave is full of tents, and down at the bottom there's an open area where humans and various creatures are gathering.

To explore the tents, turn to **63**.

To go and mingle with the people, turn to **351**.

247

The minotaur's eyes grow wide. *"You are strong... not just for a goblin – but by any common standard. All this time, you have had such power at your fingertips and yet you have hardly used it?"*

"The ring scares me," you say. "I don't like it."

"And you are right to mislike it," she intones. *"If you had used it more, it would have begun to consume you entirely, and I would have been obliged to kill you to prevent you doing evil – as I have killed so many other ringbearers."* She glances down at the pile of skulls and falls silent.

"So... does that mean you're letting me go?" you ask. "No fight?"

"Pass, ringbearer," she says. *"You are but a feeble goblin and will never resist the Smith's foul promises. But leave with my blessing all the same."* The ghost begins to fade away.

Make a note of GOLDENHEART'S BLESSING in your LOG BOOK. If you fail a skill roll, you can reverse the outcome and succeed instead. After you've used the blessing once, cross it out.

Turn to **288**.

248

You reach into the green water and grab the egg. When you pick it up, the water drains from the basin and gurgles away. The egg stops glowing as soon as it touches the air. Its shell is dark and hard and you think you can feel something moving around inside it. Tucking it into your pocket, you retrace your steps back to the entrance and head down the stairs.

Add the MYSTERIOUS EGG to your LOG BOOK
and turn to **120**.

249

The tent is filled with the scent of burning herbs and the soft glow of flickering candles. You feel awkward walking on the deep, brightly patterned carpets in your muddy shoes. The lady gestures for you to sit on a cushion and slowly folds herself down beside you to blow some life into the glowing coals of a fire. As she rearranges her shawls you take a look at her face: you don't think you've ever seen anyone so wrinkled. She says nothing as she brings out a teapot and two cups, then heats you a brew on the fire. Each movement is patient and precise as she grinds herbs and then whisks them into a froth before adding the boiling water.

"Drink this, ringbearer," she says. "I've no doubt your journey has been hard."

She holds out a simple white porcelain cup. The first sip you take is so pure that your eyes go wide in shock and you see her smile. Add 2 LIFE points. When you've finished, she settles herself, her eyes fixed upon yours.

"Can I see it?" she says. As you hold out the Night Ring, fear flickers across her face and she doesn't take it from your hand.

"You don't even want to touch it?" you ask. "I came all this way to give it to you."

"No, ringbearer," she says solemnly. "I never want to lay a finger on that wretched thing."

"Then what do you want? What should I do?" you ask.

"I am forbidden to tell you," she sighs. "For that very act might change the future. This must be a path you walk alone, ringbearer. Such are the laws of fate and the grave peril of foresight. But I do have something that may offer some of the help I cannot give..." She pulls out a small box and places it on the carpet in front of you.

"But can't you tell me about this prophecy and... and all that?" you say.

"I will tell you as much as I can," she replies. "Which is but little, I regret to say. But first look at the box. Can you open it?"

The box is decorated with lots of little scenes, several of which seem to show a blacksmith's forge. Perhaps the secret of how to open it is hidden in those pictures? Look at the picture on the next page. If you can work out the three-digit code that you need to enter to open the box, turn to that entry.

If you can't work out the code, turn to **294**.

250

The ground begins to slope upwards, and after a few minutes you climb above the mist. It stretches behind you like a blanket, while ahead of you rise hills covered in ferns and bracken.

"*Not far now!*" says a familiar voice, as a green shape appears in front of you.

"Boggo!" you exclaim, feeling glad to see him. "You won't believe what–"

"*No time,*" he interrupts. "*Tell me later. The Master's looking mighty hard for you, and if I stick around here you'll be easier to spot. So I can't linger, but I came now cos I got to warn you – he's marching an army to smash Crow Cave. You gotta move fast now. Get there before they do!*"

He starts to fade.

"Boggo, wait!" you call, but he's gone. You sigh and quicken your pace, casting an anxious glance behind you. Halfway up the first hill, it starts to rain.

Turn to **213**.

251

The creature charges and strikes you full in the chest, knocking you off your feet. You take one last look at the green leaves above before it bites through your throat.

252

You scamper away to a quiet corner and gobble up your snack. The crispy shells crack between your teeth, releasing a hot surge of spicy beetle goodness.

Add 2 LIFE points.

"Seeing you chomping that food – it's the first time I'm sad to be dead," Boggo chuckles. *"Always loved a good beetle. Time to go though."*

Midge is still chopping onions. Trying not to be noticed, you head across the kitchen towards her.

Turn to **28**.

253

You don't want to take the risk of using the ring again, so you twist away from the guard-ghoul and jab hard at its belly. The monster wasn't expecting you to move that fast and you slip out of its grip. But you're trapped between the ghoul and the water and there's nowhere to run.

"Silly goblin," it hisses. *"You can't win this fight."* It steps towards you slowly. You edge backwards wishing you could swim better as it grins and lashes out with its sword.

GUARD-GHOUL

Rounds: 5 Damage: 2

YOU

If you win, turn to **132**.

If you lose, turn to **277**.

254

With a terrible, grinding howl of metal, the cart judders to a stop. The noise echoes out into the huge cavern below.

Gain 1 ABILITY point and turn to **307**.

255

You walk as quickly as you dare along the track. As far as you can tell, the bat-riders don't seem to be interested in you yet, though it can't be long until Darkmoon works out how you've escaped and sends them this way. You wonder if they have your description yet – though you doubt Darkmoon has any idea what you look like. You were just another goblin slave to him.

Blackwell village is half a mile down the road. Beneath a grey sky, the track runs gently downhill between little woods and freshly ploughed fields. A goblin farmer in a big floppy hat is plodding uphill towards you. He greets you cheerfully with a wave, and you realise that your fists are clenched tight – all you want is to keep your head down and get as far away from Darkmoon as possible. But will it look suspicious if you don't stop for a chat?

To wave back and talk to him, turn to **314**.

If you'd prefer to give him a nod and carry on without stopping, turn to **136**.

256

You hurry down the stairs – though not quite as fast as you'd like because sprinting would draw way too much attention.

"*Always in a rush!*"

The voice behind you stops you in your tracks. You know that voice.

"Boggo?"

A green-tinged ghost bobs out of a doorway and bows.

"But... but you're dead!"

"*And you're about to get caught unless you do what I say. Come in here – it's worth your while.*" Boggo's ghost points to the fancy door he's just emerged from.

"Isn't that General Starr's map room?" you stammer.

"*Sure it is.*" Boggo steps through the door, then pauses half-in, half-out. "*Don't worry! I've unlocked it for you.*"

To follow Boggo into the Map Room, turn to **102**.

To ignore Boggo and carry on down the stairs, turn to **212**.

257

As you set off again, shaking with relief, you notice a metal tube glinting in the long grass – it must have fallen from the bat-rider's pocket during the fight. It's a silver whistle, decorated with bat wings, but when you try to blow into it, really softly, to test it, you can't hear anything. Your heart still hammering, you hurry up the hill to the waystone. Just as you'd hoped, various destinations and directions have been scratched into the old lichen-speckled stone, including one arrow marked Crow Cave that points down a sloping track towards the wooded valley. You scramble down the hill, eager to be under cover of the trees. Soon their branches are overhead and you breathe a little easier.

Add the BAT WHISTLE to your LOG BOOK and turn to **276**.

258

Sprinting hard, you jump and scramble over the blocks of shattered stone littering the street, but the orb has no difficulty keeping up with you. It floats steadily over every obstacle, squelching as it squeezes through gaps.

"*We aren't going to shake it,*" shouts Boggo. "*Need to hide.*"

As you dash around the next corner you duck through a doorway and fold yourself into the shadows just before the orb appears. Staying entirely still, you hope for the best.

Roll one dice and add it to your SNEAK level.

If your total is 5 or higher, turn to **319**.

If your total is 4 or lower, turn to **27**.

259

"*You've been enjoying my ring, I see.*" The Iron Smith's voice speaks in your head again. "*Quite the havoc you've caused.*"

"Enjoying's not the word," you say. "It's horrible."

"*It is the mirror of its bearer,*" says the voice. "*In any case it has helped you well enough. It will not help you again until you have lit my forge.*"

You remove the ring. "Why should I light your forge?" you mutter.

"What's in it for me?"

"*If my forge is lit, my fierce young friend,*" says the Iron Smith, "*I shall awake. And then perhaps I can help you in your battle. But hurry, ringbearer. The sorcerer and his hordes will soon be here.*" The voice fades, leaving you alone in the darkness, the silence broken only by the sound of something roaring down below.

Turn to **26**.

260

"*It's your lucky day, ringbearer,*" says the lizard ghost. "*I can sense you're someone who isn't afraid to use big power when they're given it. I like that, so I'm going to help you. Take a look inside that monster's stomach. You can keep whatever you find.*"

You cross the sandy arena to the giant skeleton and poke gingerly about in its ribcage. Sure enough, the bones of a lizard-woman are jumbled about inside it. Clutched in the lizard skeleton's bony fingers is a metal ball that looks a bit like a pineapple.

"*That's it,*" says the ghost, who has followed you. "*My last grenado! Take it and use it wisely.*"

Add the GRENADO to your LOG BOOK.

The grenado is a powerful magic weapon, but it can only be used once. If you throw it at an opponent in a fight it will instantly explode and do 4 Combat points of damage. Once you've used it, delete it from your LOG BOOK.

"*Goodbye, ringbearer,*" says the ghost as she wanders off into the ruins. "*May you fare better than I did...*"

Turn to **39**.

261

Boggo vanishes without a word as you move away from his house. There are howls and shouts coming from all over the village now, and you can smell burning straw. You know this mayhem is all because of you. But you also know that you can't stop to help these goblins because it's all for nothing if you don't survive. How can you get out of here? A boat, you think. But reaching the river is not going to be easy.

Turn to **195**.

262

Thinking quickly, you grab the blanket from your sack and drape it over your boat. In the darkness, it should be enough to hide any glint of metal or wood that might give away your position. The long boat passes on, and its drums dim into the distance. You lie low for a bit longer, then untie the boat and rejoin the river. The current is swift and in time you find yourself beneath the looming shadows of Rocklaw Bridge. You jump ashore, leaving the boat to drift away down the river.

Gain 1 ABILITY point and turn to **353**.

263

You duck and roll at the last moment and the cat sails overhead, screeching in surprise. Jumping for the door, you slam it shut.

Turn to **85**.

264

You've hardly gone twenty paces before the ground shakes and something gigantic slips between the trees and unfolds itself in the middle of the road. Too awestruck to run, you jump back and try to make sense of the thing that's now towering above you. It seems to be a dragon made from branches, vines and bark, as though it was born out of the forest itself.

"IT'S OFTEN THOUGHT A MISTAKE TO ENTER MY FOREST WITHOUT A SENSE OF DIRECTION," it says.

You swallow hard – it takes all your courage not to run away. "Thank you for setting me on the right path," you say, trying to keep your voice calm. "I'm very grateful."

"IT IS NO DIFFICULTY," booms the tree dragon, suddenly bending its head down towards you with the swift grace of a snake. "BUT I MUST ALSO GIVE YOU A WARNING: HARM NOTHING IN THIS FOREST... OR I WILL HARM YOU. KEEP WALKING THAT WAY AND YOU WILL REACH YOUR CAVES." It stands up to its full height again, and points down the road. "AND KEEP WATCH FOR A YOUNG SAPLING WHO IS HIDING FROM ME. I WOULD BE GRATEFUL TO BE REUNITED WITH HIM."

Just as suddenly as it came, the tree dragon slides away into the trees and disappears in a rustle of branches.

Turn to **2**.

265

You climb away from the hornets as fast as you dare… and to your intense relief they ignore you. Inching carefully downwards on the vines, you see a large balcony garden filled with big flowers in pots. Finally, you are low enough to jump down.

Turn to **287**.

266

Bracing your feet against the step, you clasp the bellows handle with both hands and bend your back. With a gradual creaking groan, the ancient leather cracks and folds. The giant arm begins to pump up and down, and the regular blasts of air from the bellows fan the furnace flames white hot.

"*Noble goblin!*" cries the Iron Smith. "*We advance!*"

Turn to **237**.

267

You jump into the minecart, which is half-full of shattered rocks and has several levers at the front. When you manage to release the rusty brake, the old metal squeaks as the cart rumbles forward. You gradually speed up, but the ancient track is cleverly designed, with little bumps and regular rises, so you never spin out of control.

"*I hope you're enjoying this,*" says Boggo grinning from ear to ear as you whistle down the track. "*I think you should listen to me more.*"

Rolling deeper under the mountain, you shoot past mineshafts and corridors and forks in the track, but keep heading straight on. You turn to ask Boggo a question, but he's pointing ahead with a very worried expression on his face... and when you look ahead again you see a pile of fallen rocks in the middle of the track. It's getting nearer extremely fast.

"*Do something!*" screams Boggo.

Just before the rocks there's a track forking off to the left, and another to the right. You have half a second to make your choice...

If you want to pull the left-hand lever, turn to **107**.

If you want to pull the right-hand lever, turn to **14**.

268

As soon as the ring is off your finger, you can feel that Darkmoon knows where you are. Boggo's father somehow seems to know the danger you're in, because he rows desperately down the river into the darkness, panting and cursing under his breath. On you row, faster and faster, until suddenly you hear a voice overhead.

"You've given us a pretty little hunt, goblin."

You look up and see the Master riding a war griffon, smiling down at you as if this was all some funny joke.

"But now it's over, I'm afraid." He points and pale fire shoots from his hand.

"Just like Boggo," you think. It's the last thought you ever have.

269

It's all you can do to cling on as Iron Mane sweeps down towards the bat-riders. They spin away from its hooves and its icy breath, but their arrows still fizz past you in the wind. You want to close your eyes as the horse swings around again for another attack, but you're aware that one lucky shot from a bat-rider could knock you off and send you tumbling to the ground far below. So you keep them wide open as the great iron horse slams straight into the riders. Several of them are killed instantly and you see their bodies plummet, while the others flee across the battlefield. Hovering now in a sudden silence, you hear the rumble and clash of battle from below.

Turn to **119**.

270

"You're lying, goblin. I can smell the fear on you."

Before you can say anything, General Starr's wand is in his hand. It glows red and as he brings it towards your throat the heat it throws off burns your skin. You open your mouth to explain yourself but one flick of the wand sends your unconscious body tumbling down the steps. You're dead before you reach the bottom.

271

As the cart smashes through the fencing at the end of the line, you jump blindly into the darkness, thudding into another cart and tumbling to a stop. The cart you were in clatters straight over the edge and disappears. Your head is buzzing, and you're seeing stars.

"Would you look at that – our beautiful ride just dived into a flamin' river of lava down there," announces Boggo, peering over the edge. "Good decision to jump, I'd say." Dusting yourself off, you check to see if anything is broken – but apart from a bump on your head, all seems well.

Deduct 1 WITS point and turn to **307**.

272

You duck into the maze of boxes, barrels and shelves. There's very little light here – it's a good place to hide, though you know you can't stay for too long. You crouch in a corner and close your eyes for a moment.

"What were you thinking?" says a voice in your head. Only it's not your voice – it's Boggo's. You look up and see Boggo's ghost perched on a box in front of you. He's a little see-through and glows faint green.

"You were always the careful one! And then you go and steal the master's ring! What a madness!" Boggo whistles between his teeth.

"Keep it down!" you hiss.

"No one else can hear me, don't fret," says Boggo.

"You're dead!" you whisper. "Aren't you?"

"I think so. And you need to get moving if you don't want to end up the same."

You know he's right. But move where? Even if you get out of the tower, you're surrounded by the Master's army. You've stolen one of his most powerful artifacts and he won't stop until he's found you. As if he's heard your question, Boggo coughs. *"If I was you, I'd get out of this tower as quick as I could, then speed like a greased eel to those rebels in Crow Cave. Lucky that Darkmoon told us where they were, eh?"*

Boggo was killed for that piece of information, you realise.

"Of course, he's obviously trying to get there too," he continues. *"So you'd have to be right speedy to get there first. But then maybe with the power of that ring the rebels might stand a chance of beating him?"* Boggo pauses, as if struck by something. *"By the way,"* he whispers. *"What does it actually do?"*

"The ring?" You shrug your shoulders. "I'm no magician."

Boggo clicks his tongue thoughtfully. *"Well anyway, it must be something powerful or it wouldn't have been on that shelf. Now then, if I was you I'd have a rummage around this storeroom to find something you can use."*

You nod. Boggo's suddenly talking a lot of sense. He's never done that before. Is that what happens when you die? Picking through the storeroom, you find a few items that might be useful, and a sack big enough to hold three of them.

Pick three items from this list and add them to your LOG BOOK: a ROPE, a TINDER BOX, a FLASK OF OIL, a BLANKET, and a COMPASS.

To stay here for a while and look for a weapon, turn to **338**.

To hurry on and try to escape, turn to **85**.

273

For a long while, you row down the river, fully expecting Darkmoon to appear, take back his ring, and blast you into tiny pieces. But to your great surprise you seem to have given him the slip, again. At last, you see the shattered blocks of Rocklaw Bridge looming ahead of you. You jump onto the steep bank and kick your boat out into the current so that no one will know that you've come ashore here. You don't know how close the hunt is, but you aren't taking any chances.

Turn to **353**.

274

Away to your left in the centre of the enemy army a giant war elephant is thundering along. It carries a swaying platform on its back, tall and turreted like a castle.

"*Within that beast's wooden fortress is the one you seek,*" says the Smith. "*I smell him.*"

Flags are waving from the upper deck above the war elephant and bright flares are being fired from inside it. When the enemy hordes see the flares, they all turn to look at Iron Mane and start to fire their weapons up at you – Darkmoon must have ordered his army to focus on the winged horse.

"*You will have only one chance at this,*" growls the Iron Smith. "*Ready your arm.*"

You speed just above the helmets of the army. You're going far too fast for them to hit you with their spears, although a few arrows buzz uncomfortably close. Iron Mane is weaving, dodging the wild blasts of magic that shoot from the elephant's fortress and smash into

Darkmoon's own soldiers when they miss.

"*Lift your weapon!*" orders the Smith. As you do, you feel an iron strength flowing into your arm, locking it tight. Iron Mane feints as if to rise and shoot over the top of the castle, and then at the last moment it dives down between the elephant's churning legs.

Roll one dice and add your STRENGTH level, your SNEAK level and your WITS level.

If the total is 14 or higher, turn to **126**.

If the total is 13 or lower, turn to **148**.

275

Lizardfolk consider themselves the cleverest and most senior of Darkmoon's servants. They're far too important to be bossed around by hobtoads, and they'd never usually speak to a goblin. So maybe you can use their arrogance against them: if you can get them into an argument with the guards, you might slip out while everyone is distracted. They don't even look at you as you sidle closer.

"Utterly outrageous," says a tall one in midnight-blue robes. He clacks his claws together irritably. "Did you see how that toad actually set her filthy paws on my shoulder?"

"The swampy stench is what gets me," shudders the smallest and most sneery lizard. She's wearing a pointy hat, which means she's very important indeed. You cough discreetly.

"What is it goblin?" she snorts.

You pause for a second, thinking fast. You know two things about lizardfolk that just might be useful here: they prize their appearance above all things, and they never show their faces in public.

To tell the lizardfolk that the hobtoads are planning to ask them to remove their masks, turn to **90**.

To tell the lizardfolk that the hobtoads are laughing at how they look, turn to **184**.

276

You stride round a corner and stop dead in your tracks. There, right before you, is the shimmering vision you last saw in Darkmoon's mirror. Only this time it's real and smells of pine needles and spring grass. Crow Cave is exactly the same: the tall, round-sided hill that rises at the end of the valley, and the waterfall that emerges from a wide cave in the hillside and tumbles like a thin line of white paint into the misty lake. At the top of the hill squats the same ruined fortress, but you can see that the path you're on isn't heading there, but to the cavemouth. It's a wide track, built of old stone slabs and clearly in regular use. Near the cavemouth there's a heap of rocks by the side of the track, and just beyond it you spot several guards in helmets watching the road – rebels!

"*Nice one!*" whispers a faint, familiar voice in your ear. "*Now finish the job.*"

When you turn around there's no sign of Boggo. For a moment you let your thoughts dwell on the fact that he died so that Darkmoon could find this place. You feel anger rising in you but you try to push it away – it's a cool head you need now, more than ever. There's no way you'll be able to sneak past those guards. Will they let you in? Will they even listen to a goblin? What if they just kill you on the spot? Your mind whirring, you step towards them and make your choice.

To tell the guards about the Night Ring, turn to **219**.

To talk to the guards but keep the ring a secret, turn to **309**.

277

Trapped by the river behind you, there's nowhere for you to run. The guard-ghoul drives you back and back, until it strikes you down and you collapse into the dark water and never surface. Your body and the ring are carried down the river and out to sea. The ring is not found for another fifty years, when a fisherman catches it in his net. What happens next is a story for another book...

278

"I'll do it," you say.

"WELL SAID, FRIEND," says the dragon. It points into the wood. "MANY YEARS AGO, DARKMOON SENT AN ARMY HERE. WE DESTROYED THEM OF COURSE, BUT IT WAS A TRAP. FOR IN THEIR DYING, THEY RELEASED THE ROT."

It bends down so its great head is close to yours.

"FIND THE PLACE WHERE THE LAST BODY FELL. TOUCH

THE RING TO THAT CURSED SPOT, AND YOU WILL DESTROY THE SOURCE OF THE ROT."

You look at the tangle of rotten trees and the foul spread of mushrooms. You can see rusty pieces of armour and old bones sticking out of it. There's barely a safe patch of ground to stand on.

"WORRY NOT. IF YOU PUT ON THE RING, THE ROT CANNOT HARM YOU," says the dragon. "AND DARKMOON CANNOT SEE YOU INSIDE MY FOREST. I HAVE SOME POWER STILL. NOW GO! LET THE RING GUIDE YOU TO THE PLACE, AND THEN YOUR EYES MUST DO THE REST!"

You do as you're told: putting the ring on your finger, you walk straight into the rot. The dragon was right – there's something different about the ring here. You don't have the same feeling of power, and you can't feel Darkmoon looking for you. But you still see ghosts. The rotten forest is full of them, and they reach out to you as you pass.

"*Release us... ringbearer,*" they whisper. "*Set us free...*"

You can feel the ring tugging you in a particular direction and you let it guide you. There's no way to avoid touching the rot, but with the ring on it doesn't harm you, as the dragon promised. Eventually you arrive at a patch of broken forest thickly tangled with rot, and the ring begins trembling on your finger. You must be near the source, but there are so many twisting strands of rot that it's hard to know where to look. Holding your breath against the stink, you walk in deeper. The ring seems to buzz hardest when you're close to the low-hanging branch of an apple tree.

Look at the picture on the next page. If you can work out where the source of the rot is, turn to the number that is revealed.

If you can't find the source, turn to **19**.

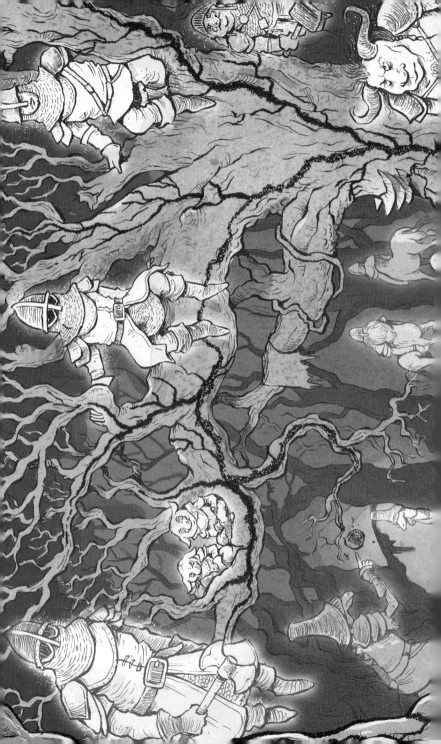

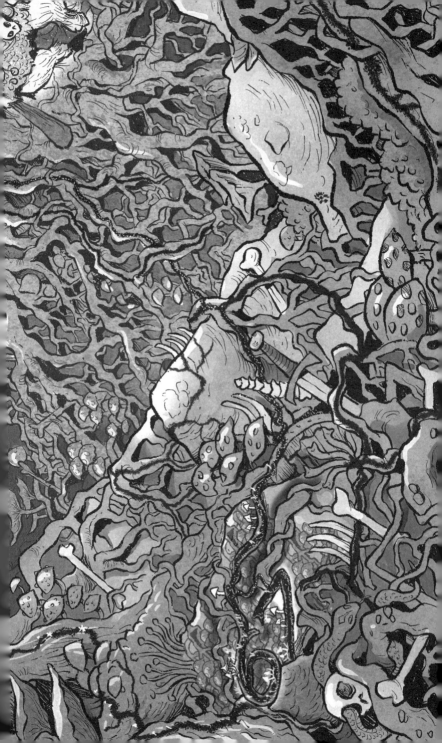

As Darkmoon is conjuring another spell, Iron Mane dives in. The wizard launches a crackling surge of pale fire from his fingertips, but the horse flies straight through it, aiming directly for Darkmoon's heart. As you crash into him, you strike his head with all your strength and Iron Mane sends a lightning bolt flashing from his hoof. The impact sends the wizard flying, and as you zoom away you glance down at him. With a startled expression, Darkmoon is struggling to rise to his knees, then his head droops and he sprawls lifeless on the mud. Iron Mane lands nearby, and you become aware of what's happening around you again. Your enemies are fleeing the battlefield as the iron army marches unstoppably forwards. You can hear the faint cheers of the rebels in the distance, almost drowned out by the metallic clanking of the soldiers who saved your life.

Boggo is looking down at Darkmoon's corpse. He raises his eyes to meet yours. "*I know you did all this because you wanted to save everyone from him,*" he says. "*Because it was the right thing to do. But I reckon you sort of did it for me as well.*" You exchange a long look with your best friend. Suddenly, you feel very tired.

"*A decent day's work, ringbearer,*" says the Iron Smith as he steps out of Iron Mane, who turns back into a statue. Only a thin sliver of sun remains above the hills and his pale ghost is frosted with golden light. "*The tale of this fight will be told for all time – but perhaps it is only the first of your many glories. What shall we do now? The iron army stands ready for your next command!*"

You look at the ring. It's hard to imagine that such a little thing could cause so much mayhem and destruction.

"*Just imagine what we can build together...*" whispers the Smith.

"I don't know," you say. It's hard to forget all the ghosts you've met along the way and their pleas to be released – if you destroy the ring, do you set them free?

"*Don't be a fool!*" urges the Smith. "*Don't you see? If you break my ring, you break everything. You will have no power – you will be normal again. Boring. Just an average little goblin who once got lucky and stumbled into an adventure.*"

You hesitate, and the Smith plays his last card. "*If you destroy the ring, you will lose Boggo forever. You will never speak to him again. He will truly die and be gone from this world, and then all your striving will count for nothing.*"

You hadn't really considered that possibility. When you look at Boggo, he has a gentle smile on his face. "*I know you'll make the right choice,*" he says. "*You always do.*"

You look down at the ring again, sitting on the palm of your hand.

To destroy the ring, turn to **32**.

To keep the ring, turn to **283**.

280

You dive out of the way of the plant's gigantic bite, snatching up the whistle as you go.

Roll one dice and add your STRENGTH level and your SNEAK level.

If your total is 7 or higher, turn to **203**.

If your total is 6 or lower, turn to **70**.

281

"*Pah!*" sneers the lizard ghost. "*What was stopping you using the ring more? Too scared? I like creatures who are brave enough to take power when it's offered, not throw it away. When you fail – and you will fail – you'll be stuck here with me, cursed forever.*"

She wanders off behind a broken column, leaving you alone.

"*Not all ghosts are as nice as me,*" whispers Boggo.

Turn to **39**.

282

You try to run, but the cat backs you against the wall and slashes at your face. You dodge as best you can, but its massive paws and dripping jaws are relentless. It leans in and takes a big bite out of your shoulder, and as you roar in pain you bash it on the nose as hard as you can. It yowls in surprise, and you duck out of the door, slamming it behind you.

Deduct 1 LIFE point and turn to **85**.

283

You look at the ring for a long time as a breeze stirs the grass of the moonlit battlefield. Then you put it in your pocket. It's too precious and powerful to waste, and you know that you'll be able to use it to do good. Giving Boggo a grin, you start the long trudge home.

One year later, you are the new ruler of the land. With the Iron Smith always by your side, you use the iron army to crush anyone who disagrees with you. Soon your power is absolute. Very little changes for the people, except that now it's goblins who are in charge rather than humans. You move back into Darkmoon's tower and rename it after Boggo, but as your rule continues you see him less and less. Busy with conquering your new empire you don't notice him fading into the background. On the day when you replace the paintings in Darkmoon's picture gallery with pictures of yourself, you realise that you haven't seen him for months – and when you summon him, he only says one thing.

"*You should have broken that ring.*"

284

The griefers seem to be having an argument – they're muttering and snarling and pushing each other around. This allows you to sneak along the bridge and get quite close without being spotted, but there's no way you'll get right past them to the forge. They're drinking from a bucket that they pass around, and when it's empty one of them refills it from a big barrel near the bridge. Thinking quickly, you wait until they're looking the other way, uncork the LAUGHING SYRUP, lean over the edge and empty it into the barrel. Then you flatten yourself onto the bridge and wait to see what happens. After a while one of them refills the bucket from the barrel and takes a big gulp. As soon as the liquid hits his mouth, he starts to choke, then great snorts of laughter shake his body. He falls to the ground and the others crowd around him, grabbing the bucket and drinking it dry. Soon they're all collapsed on the floor, sniggering uncontrollably. You walk past without even trying to hide, and they do nothing but laugh.

Gain 1 ABILITY point and turn to **64**.

285

Steadily stepping down and down, you get the feeling that you must be nearly at the base of the tower, though there's no end to the darkness yet. You walk carefully, watching out for further traps. Around the corner you start to see a faint green glow on the bricks, and soon you spot an opening in the wall with light pouring through it. You edge closer and peer into a small room. Beautiful pictures of dragons made from thousands of tiny tiles cover the walls. The dragons are shown flying and fighting in complicated patterns. In the centre of the room is a stone basin carved into the shape of a nest. The green, glowing water that fills the basin is where the light is coming from, and there's what looks like a large egg bobbing about inside it. The floor of the room is thick with dust – and you can see a set of footprints in it. Someone seems to have taken a strange, hopping path to the basin and back again.

To follow the footsteps to the basin, turn to **163**.

To ignore the footsteps and take a different path to the basin, turn to **52**.

To walk on past the room and hurry down the stairs, turn to **120**.

286

"Erm, hello?" you say.

The dragon doesn't stir. Half-buried by the dust and rubble of a shattered mansion, its great flanks rise and fall with every breath. You're suddenly aware of how old this creature must be and how long it may have been asleep.

"*I don't think that's how you talk to a dragon,*" says Boggo.

"They're mighty things! You have to be more polite and use long words."

The dragon opens a single yellow eye. "I DON'T CARE FOR CEREMONY, LITTLE BUG."

Boggo squeaks and jumps behind you. *"I didn't think it could hear me!"*

"WHAT DO YOU WANT WITH ME?" The dragon's voice is a growl of distant thunder, and flames flicker at its nostrils. "SPEAK QUICKLY AND WELL. I'M FAMISHED – I HAVEN'T EATEN IN TWO HUNDRED YEARS."

Roll one dice and add your WITS level and your STRENGTH level.

If your total is 11 or higher, turn to **231**.

If your total is 10 or lower, turn to **330**.

287

The balcony you're standing on is full of big, strange plants in pots. Their roots snake across the floor, and huge flowers covered in pointy teeth loom over you. You notice that each pot has a tube connected to it, all leading to a large barrel in the corner. A wooden board has been nailed to the wall, and a strange symbol has been painted on it – it looks like a whistle, with "zzzzz" coming out of it. Below the sign, you spot a pruning blade that's been abandoned on a bench and pick it up.

Add the PRUNING BLADE to your LOG BOOK – it's a weapon, so you no longer have to subtract 1 from all your rolls in a fight.

As you tuck the weapon into your belt, you glimpse a body on the ground, half-hidden in the corner.

To try to find a way off the balcony, turn to **4**.

To investigate the body, turn to **87**.

To take a closer look at the plants, turn to **145**.

288

Your thoughts return to the rebels somewhere above as you step quickly up the iron stairs, your footsteps echoing on the metal. The forge's doors open silently as you approach and you walk through into a vast, gloomy chamber with an unlit furnace shaped like a pyramid in the centre of it. In the distance, you can see what looks like a giant water wheel. The Iron Smith's smooth voice rings out in your head again.

"*You have done well to come so far, ringbearer – so many have failed. But three final challenges await if you are to restart this forge of mine. Do you see that glow over there?*"

You scan the room, and your eyes make out the gleam of something red on the far wall.

"*Your first task awaits you there,*" says the Smith. "*Prove yourself worthy of my power.*"

Turn to **84**.

You reach into your pocket and fumble for the ring. As soon as you touch it you feel a spark, and then somehow it slides up onto your finger.

"Stop there, goblin!" shouts the guard. You do stop – but not because you've been ordered to. As soon as the ring's on your finger, you suddenly see a different world. In the shadows, thin shapes reach out to you. Shadows made of bone, rags, scraps of fur and skin. They're all ghosts, you realise – ghosts of goblins, humans, hobtoads and beasts.

"*Help us, ringbearer!*" they whisper. "*Free us, ringbearer!*"

You don't know how to free them, but you can feel that you have some kind of power over them. It's surging through you like lightning – a thunderboom, just like Boggo said. As the guards stride towards you, you raise the hand with the ring on it.

"Hold them..." you order, a little uncertainly, pointing at the hobtoads. The ghosts immediately do your bidding, swarming the startled guards and freezing them in place. Frost crackles around their bodies, and ice spreads across their skin. Squealing with horror, the hobtoads are powerless to resist. You don't know what you were expecting to happen, though it certainly wasn't this. But you seize your chance and hurry past. As you're jogging towards the daylight at the end of the tunnel, you suddenly get the strange feeling that someone is looking at you. Then you hear a voice – Darkmoon's voice – echoing in your head, and you realise the ring has drawn him straight to you.

"You!" he says. He starts to laugh. "A little goblin. Using MY ring? Believe me, it would be far better to give up now. I promise to make your death short and swift. But know, if you continue to defy me, I will find you and..."

Before he can say any more, you pull the ring from your finger and stuff it back in your pocket. Darkmoon's sneers instantly disappear from your head. You realise you're going to have to be very careful using the ring in the future.

Turn to **215**.

290

You don't spot the needlegrass until you walk right into a patch of it and a searing pain in your shins makes you look down. Several of the razor-sharp stems have sliced through your boots, drawing blood. Wishing you'd listened more carefully to your grandpa's nature chats when you were just a tiny goblin cub, you staunch the bleeding and limp on towards Blackwell.

Deduct 1 LIFE point and turn to **147**.

291

The monster reaches you quickly. Maybe it was once a bear, but now it's some kind of zombie held together with rot and scraps of skin. As it rears up on its hind legs and bites for your head, all you can see are bone-white teeth flecked with bloody foam.

ZOMBIE BEAR

Rounds: 4   Damage: 2

YOU

If you win the fight, turn to **349**.

If you lose, turn to **251**.

292

You slip the golden tunic over your clothes and pull the hood low over your face. When you step out of the tent no one gives you a second look. The crowd seems to be flowing down towards the open space in the middle of the tents where people are gathering. You follow, keeping your eyes to yourself, and find a quiet spot to crouch and wait. The rebels look scared and tired, but the hum of worried chatter stops when an old lady climbs on top of a barrel and raises her hands for silence.

"My friends," she says, her voice quiet but authoritative. "I know the shadows of doubt and fear have crept into your hearts. We are cornered, and our enemy will soon be here. But I believe the prophecy still holds. I believe the ringbearer will come. And then, though the way ahead will remain dark and dangerous, hope can burn in our hearts again."

Ringbearer. You've been called that before, but is she really talking about you? Is it you they're waiting for?

"*Hey ringbearer!*" says Boggo, appearing beside you. He waggles his eyebrows. *"So how are you going to make your entrance and tell them all you're here? I say, the more dramatic the better!"*

If you want to make a dramatic entrance, turn to **13**.

If you want to be more discreet, turn to **160**.

293

"SUPERGROWTH FORMULA" is stamped in large letters on the side of the barrel. Tubes run from the barrel to every plant pot, and there's a little tap on the side of it. When you turn the tap, a glowing green liquid drips out.

To drink some of the liquid, turn to **81**.

To try and find a way off the balcony, turn to **4**.

294

"I can't do it," you say, and put down the box. The old lady can't hide her disappointment, or the doubt that creeps into her eyes.

"The ring chose you," she says, mustering a smile. "I must not worry, because when the time comes you will rise to the challenge. I was foolish to try even this little gesture to nudge events in your favour. This is a sign from the goddess that I must respect your destiny."

"So you won't help?" you ask.

"It would be foolish, after that message," she mumbles. She sighs and gets to her feet. "Come. All I can do is set you on your path."

Deduct 1 WITS point and turn to **339**.

295

"What are you doing?" hisses Boggo as you examine the wall of weapons. Most of them look too big and heavy for you to use, but three of them immediately catch your eye: a CRYSTAL PICK like an icicle, a SMALL HAND-AXE with a glowing rune carved into the handle and a serrated WAR UMBRELLA.

"Come on, pick one and get out of here!" urges Boggo.

When you've made your choice turn to **152**.

296

"ATCHOOOOOOO!" You can't stop the volcanic sneeze from bursting out of your nose. Immediately you hear Boggo's mum screaming upstairs as the chest is dragged aside. Suddenly the trapdoor is open and bright light is streaming down on you. As soldiers lean down into your hiding place you know there's only one way to stay alive, and you just have time to slip the ring onto your finger.

"HOLD THEM!" you growl, feeling the surge of power inside you and pointing up at your enemies. At once, every soldier is frozen to the spot. Their frightened eyes follow you as you climb out of the smuggler's hole. Boggo's parents look terrified too.

"There's no time to explain it to them. Got to get out of here," says Boggo. *"You're glowing like a beacon all over again. Darkmoon's going to see you! But make sure the soldiers can't remember any of this. Or they'll kill Mum and Dad for sure."*

You flash him a questioning look.

"Use the ring! Use its power!" Boggo urges.

Hesitantly you clear your throat, and then you say in a loud voice that doesn't feel like your own: "GO AWAY. NEVER SPEAK OF THIS AGAIN." The soldiers run silently from the room, and Boggo's mum starts to weep. But worse, somewhere far away, you feel Darkmoon notice what you've done. You pull the ring from your finger.

"You better leave," says Boggo's dad. He sounds angry or scared – you can't tell which it is, maybe both. "Take my boat. It's tied up below. Go!" He hurries you down to the riverside and pushes you into a little rowing boat. Then he unties the rope and shoves you out into the current.

"Now get out of here!" he shouts. As you float down the river, Blackwell village burns.

Colour in a section of the RING TRACKER on your LOG BOOK, then roll one dice.

If the number is equal to or lower than your RING SCORE, turn to **6**.

If the number is higher than your RING SCORE, turn to **178**.

297

You try to pull the ring from your finger, but it won't come off. It seems to be stuck, as though it's glued to your skin. You're still tugging at it when a familiar voice speaks quietly behind you.

"That's my ring, goblin."

You turn around just in time to see the pale fire that blasts your head off your body.

298

Wherever you dodge there's another mouth waiting to gobble you up, and as you desperately fend off the griefers you know the end can't be far away. One of them lunges towards you, giggling with delight, but it trips over one of the others who is lying on the ground. Howling with anger, your attacker turns to attack its fallen friend instead, and before you know it a savage fight has broken out among the beasts, who ignore you for a moment. You sneak away, amazed that you've somehow survived.

Gain 1 ABILITY point and turn to **64**.

299

To your relief, there are no more obstacles on the track. The mineshafts open out into bigger caves filled with buildings, and rooms carved into the mountain. You pass a huge stone table still set for an enormous meal, and then a playground with long slides cut into the rock. Everything is covered in thick dust.

"*Not a bad place to live!*" says Boggo admiringly. The track flattens suddenly and you shoot out into a big open space. Then Boggo starts to scream...

"*The brakes! The brakes! Pull the brakes!*"

You glimpse a vast cavern far below you with rivers of lava running through it, and the streets of a city between them – but you don't have much time to take in the view because the minecart is rushing towards a very big drop. The void is opening up ahead of you, waiting to swallow you up, and there's no way you'd survive this fall. Grabbing the brake, you squeeze your eyes shut and pull...

Roll one dice and add it to your STRENGTH level.

If your total is 6 or higher, turn to **254**.

If your total is 5 or lower, turn to **91**.

300

You haven't gone far when a jumble of bones by the side of the track gathers itself together and lurches to its feet. It's a strange and terrifying mix of different creatures: a minotaur's skull, a human's ribcage and a goblin's spindly legs. You've no choice but to defend yourself as it rattles and staggers towards you, waving a rusty sword.

MISMATCHED SKELETON

Rounds: 4   Damage: 2

YOU

If you win, turn to **317**.

If you lose, turn to **96**.

301

You creep along the bridge, trying to crouch low and scurrying as quickly as you can. Fortunately the griefers are far too interested in squabbling with each other to notice you yet. They are refilling a bucket from a large barrel marked STINGO and passing it around, pouring the liquid straight down their throats. As you creep a little closer, you realise it would be almost impossible to sneak past them – there's no cover, and the path to the forge lies directly beyond them. You're going to need a plan.

Roll one dice and add it to your WITS level.

If your total is 5 or higher, turn to **162**.

If your total is 4 or lower, turn to **348**.

302

Standing on the red-tiled roof, you look about at all the chimneys and angled slopes – you're not sure exactly where you are or where to go. It feels very exposed up here – anyone watching from above would be sure to see you, and that thought makes you check the sky. Looking back up at the huge bulk of the tower, you see a winged creature launching from the tallest spire, then another, and another. Each one has a tiny figure clinging to its back. With a shudder, you realise that Darkmoon's bat-riders are joining the hunt for you. You duck back into the shadows, hoping one hasn't spotted you already.

Now it's even more important to somehow get off this roof. You glance desperately at the slopes and walls and sheer drops until you spot a cluster of smoking chimneys a few roofs down. The smoke smells of greasy meat, fiery spices and over-stewed vegetables – the unmistakable odour of the kitchen. That would be a perfect place to hide in: there'll be lots of goblins and plenty of distractions. Even better, there's a chimney sweep's door set into the side of the clump of chimneys. You try to judge how long it's going to take you to sprint down there across the rooftops. With one last glance up at the skies – all clear – you make a dash for it.

Roll one dice and add your SNEAK and your STRENGTH levels.

If your total is 7 or higher, turn to **30**.

If your total is 6 or lower, turn to **114**.

303

You climb up among the wheels to investigate the problem, but the metal is slippery and as you inch towards the blockage you lose your footing and slip into the cascading water. For a few hair-raising moments the torrent is all over you, threatening to send you plummeting back to the ground, but you manage to pull yourself back up to safety. Cursing, you clamber above the blockage and take a few deep breaths. When you pat yourself down you notice with a curse that some of your belongings have been washed away. It doesn't take you long to fix the blockage though – one well-judged kick sends the debris tumbling and soon the water is flowing through the chutes as it should. At the base of the scaffolding it gurgles away into pipes that carry it out across the forge.

"*You are ready to light the furnace,*" booms the Iron Smith.

Delete any two items from your LOG BOOK, and turn to **153**.

304

You explain that you've run away from the tower after Darkmoon killed your best friend, and you can see emotion rising in the old farmer's face as he listens. In the end he refuses to accept any payment, gives you his floppy hat and coat and takes your old uniform in exchange. Your new clothes fit well, although they do smell of turnips. As you turn to leave, he calls out after you...

"A piece of advice, youngling! Watch out for magpies in the trees. Those blasted birds are Darkmoon's darlings and you can't trust 'em. Good luck to yer!"

If you meet any magpies later in your journey and you'd like to make use of the farmer's advice, add 10 to the entry you're on and turn to that number.

Add the DISGUISE to your LOG BOOK and turn to **147**.

305

"NO!" booms a voice.

Before you can raise your weapon, a gigantic trunk-like arm reaches out of the forest and slaps it out of your hand, before another limb catches the little deer-sapling and lifts it out of your reach. As you look up in shock, the trees shudder and shake and a giant creature thumps out into the road and unfolds itself to its full, enormous height. It looks like a dragon, but seems to be made from branches, vines and bark, as if the forest has come alive. You stumble away but there's no escape – the dragon is lumbering after you, clearly furious, and you know its next blow will be coming for your head.

If you want to dodge the blow, turn to **332**.

If you want to apologise, turn to **170**.

If you want to use the ring, turn to **181**.

306

You hold your breath and cling to the vines. The wind whistles around the tower and the buzzing is getting louder and louder as the hornets swarm towards you. Some are crawling across your skin and into your clothes, and then a burning needle of pain stabs the back of your thigh. You grit your teeth to stop yourself making a sound and you try to stay calm, motionless, not even blinking. Several long moments pass as the agony of the sting builds and the horrible creatures buzz about you, but somehow your grip holds and the hornets grow bored and retreat to their nest. With trembling arms you climb carefully around it. Below your feet is a balcony garden filled with plants, getting steadily closer. Finally, you are low enough to jump down.

Deduct 1 LIFE point and turn to **287**.

You stand on the edge of the drop, looking down. Several sets of wide stairs are cut into the steep cliff, so getting to the bottom won't be a problem – but the wrecked city on the cave floor below is full of smoking channels of lava and huge heaps of rubble where damaged buildings are blocking the ancient streets. The smoke swirls, and for a moment you imagine the place as it must have looked when the Iron Smith ruled here. You can picture the towers painted in brilliant colours and the bustling crowds in the markets. The smoke drifts again, and the lava-lit ruins return.

"*I think that's where we need to go,*" says Boggo, pointing towards the largest group of buildings at the far end of the cave. "*That looks like the forge.*" He's right – all the channels of lava flow into those buildings, and several tumbling waterfalls turn huge wheels that are still attached to the biggest building. Unlike the rest of the ruined city, the forge still gleams like new. But what's the fastest way to get there? Time is running out for the rebels, and you wonder if Darkmoon's armies have already reached the caves above. You frown and stare at the city. If you don't make a plan while you're standing up here, you're bound to get lost once you're down there...

Look at the picture on the next page. The city is lit by jets of flaming gas. From your starting point in the bottom left corner, what is the fewest number of jets that you can walk past to reach the Iron Smith's forge?

Multiply the number of flaming jets that you pass by 40 and turn to that entry.

If you can't work out the correct route, turn to **89**.

Your eyes start to swim as you stare at all the little labels, and you realise this is taking far too long – someone is bound to come looking for you here sooner or later. You slip out of the spice pantry as quietly as you can. Luckily, Groucho isn't watching and the kitchen is busy. As you hurry towards the cellar stairs you fail to notice a chef turning away from a stove with a cauldron of boiling oil. You narrowly avoid smashing into him, but some oil splashes over the edge and lands sizzling on your arm. Cursing silently, you look left and right then leave the kitchen.

Deduct 1 LIFE point and turn to **104**.

309

You walk up the hill, making no effort to hide yourself.

"Greetings," you say, as you approach the soldiers. "I've come–"

Before you can say any more, the heap of rocks by the track scatters and a human-sized cat springs out of it. You find yourself grabbed by the collar and lifted, legs kicking, into the air.

"Jaco! This is bold, even for a goblin!" exclaims the cat. You can smell the garlic that she ate for lunch. "The world's stupidest spy!"

"I'm not a spy!" you say, gasping as your collar starts to strangle you. "I'm on the run!"

"Yeah, yeah. That's what they all say," another guard snarls. "We'll just run you through now, eh? Save us some time." He jabs the point of his spear into your leg.

Deduct 2 LIFE points.

"Wait..." The voice comes from inside the tunnel – the kind of voice that expects to be obeyed. "Maybe there's some use in questioning the creature. Let me handle this."

The two guards hand you over to a bald man with a red scar running across his cheek. He grabs your shoulder with an iron grip and pushes you down a long passage into the cave, ignoring the side turnings. You pass creatures of all kinds who all seem to be scurrying here and there in a great hurry. A pair of otterlings raise their bushy eyebrows at the sight of you being marched past, and a centaur snorts and frowns at you. Soon you arrive in a much bigger cave, lit by the glow of the green moss that grows on the ceiling high above. Dozens of tents are clustered around a small open space at the bottom where people are gathering.

You're approaching a wide tent that's guarded by soldiers. An officer with a thick moustache is watching you curiously.

"Who's this, Longarm?" he asks.

"Caught a spy at the cave," replies the bald man. "Thought maybe you could make the goblin talk?"

"In there," snaps the officer, and shoves you into the tent.

Turn to **328**.

For a long, dreadful moment, the guard-ghoul seems to be staring right at you, but its gaze slides over you at last. It snaps an order to the rowers and they hurry on across the dark water. Soon the drums are fading into the distance.

"Fools, making all that noise!" says Boggo's dad as he unties the boat and sets off down the river. "Lucky they're as stupid as they're evil, eh?"

Soon enough, you're floating in the shadow of Rocklaw Bridge. The shattered arch looms overhead. You've never seen it before – it's huge, and you struggle to imagine the force it must have taken to break it. You heard once it was Darkmoon himself who did it, with a single stroke of his sword.

"I'll leave you here," says Boggo's dad. "And I wish you good luck. Do it for Boggo."

"Thank you," you say. "I will."

You climb up the bank as he starts to row with a steady stroke upstream.

Turn to **353**.

The hobtoad gulps.

"A demon, eh?" She blinks at you, and you can almost see the idea slowly moving through her brain – then she nods and heads warily towards the top floor. You scamper downwards, step after step, spiral after spiral and all the time all you can think is "What have I done?" Then you hear the sound of boots charging up the stairs towards you.

But that isn't the most alarming sound you hear.

"Hurry you dogs!" It's the cold voice of Marcox, your Master's butler. You've seen what he does to goblins who don't wash a glass properly, so you can't imagine what he'd do to a goblin who's stolen one of the Master's greatest treasures.

If you want to try to bluff your way past Marcox, turn to **135**.

If you want to try and hide, turn to **40**.

312

Your arms grow weary as you shift the heavy skulls from basin to basin. Eventually you sit down exhausted, and stare dejectedly at the pictures on the door.

"*To have come so far*," says the Smith. "*And yet to fail here. Above, your friends are already dying.*"

"I can't do it," you say.

"*Then someone else will*," says the Iron Smith. "*I am prepared to wait.*"

Suddenly the floor beneath you gives way and you are plunged directly into a pool of lava. You die at once as your body melts quickly away, leaving only the Night Ring to float into the channels deep beneath the mountain.

Boggo's dad is a goblin of few words, and he stares silently into the fading light as he steers the boat away from Blackwell on the fast-flowing current. No one sees you go except the fireflies that blink over the dark water.

"Where you headed, friend?" he says.

"Crow Cave."

He nods. "Goin' to visit the rebels, eh?"

You stare at him in surprise. Darkmoon has been searching for those rebels for months, but apparently their hiding place is common knowledge round here.

"Oh yes," he says, "I know where they are. Smuggled a few things to the caves, this past year: some weapons, some food, some information. No goblin's a friend of Darkmoon in Blackwell. Anyway, you must be famished. Here, have some soup."

He offers you a steaming flask of hot crab chowder. Each sip warms your belly and your bones.

Add 3 LIFE points.

"Do you know the best way to get to Crow Cave?" you ask, wiping the last of the broth from your lips. He thinks, then spits in the water. "The New Road is fastest, but it ain't safe – they'll be looking for you there. I'll set you down at Rocklaw Bridge. It's the longer way round, but they might not follow you there."

"Why not?" you ask.

He chuckles grimly. "Cos to get to Crow Cave from there, you can either take a nice little stroll through Phantom Forest or a slog through Battle Marsh – and no goblin in their right mind would want to do either."

Your journey doesn't seem to be getting any easier.

"Sorry I can't do more for you, youngster," he continues. "I wish I could help you against Darkmoon, after all the evil he's done..." His voice tails off, and you know he's thinking about Boggo.

"I'm sorry," you say. "I wish I could have stopped him."

You both stare into the darkness as the boat slips downstream. Finally he shakes himself and nods towards a pile of blankets at the back.

"Why don't you get some shut-eye?" he says. "I'll wake you as we come up to Rocklaw – it'll only be a few hours."

You suddenly realise how exhausted you are. Settling down in the back of the boat among the warm blankets, you close your eyes. The gentle rocking of the water soon sends you to sleep.

Turn to **164**.

314

"Well met, youngling," says the old goblin. He looks delighted to have someone to talk to. "Why's a fancy Tower goblin like you out here? Cold day for a stroll amongst the turnips."

You explain that you're on your way to Blackwell.

"Visitin' family, eh?" His sharp eyes peer up at you from beneath his hat. "Though I don't *recognise* your face?"

Suddenly you think how useful it would be if no one recognised you – a disguise is what you need.

"Do you think... I could borrow your jacket?" you say. "And... I really like your hat."

"Oh it's like that is it?" he laughs. "You on the run?" He sounds quite friendly, but his eyes narrow at the prospect of striking a deal – every goblin loves to bargain. You wonder if you can persuade him to help you...

Roll one dice and add it to your WITS level.

If the total is 7 or higher, turn to **304**.

If the total is 6 or lower, turn to **240**.

315

You feel the plant's jaws close around your leg. Its needle-thin teeth stab through your skin, spreading a strange numbness into your body.

Deduct 1 LIFE point and 1 STRENGTH point.

You fight the plant as you desperately struggle to free yourself from its grip. In this fight, deduct 1 from your attack rolls until you make a successful attack. If you hit it once, the plant releases you and you can swing freely and attack normally once more.

GIANT PLANT

Rounds: 5   Damage: 1

YOU

If you win, turn to **94**.

If you lose, turn to **235**.

316

"Um, excuse me," you begin, trying to mimic a human's voice, "I know things seem bleak, but–"

"Who asked you?" The bearded man's voice is tense. "Hey! Who are you anyway?"

The woman peers at you and her eyes widen with disgust. "Timor! That's a goblin! We've been infiltrated!" Their fear turns quickly to anger. They kick you to the ground, binding your hands and stuffing a sock in your mouth so you can't explain anything.

Deduct 1 LIFE point.

You're dragged through the cave to a big tent surrounded by armed guards. A smooth-looking officer with a full grey moustache looks up from his papers as you approach.

"Now what's all this about?" he says.

"We found this spy!" the humans crow. "A stinkin' goblin!"

The officer squints at you and his nostrils flare a little as he sniffs.

"Hmm. Well that certainly appears to be the case," he says. "My thanks to you, comrades. I'll take it from here." He takes you by the shoulder and shoves you into the tent.

Turn to **328**.

317

It just takes one well-placed wallop for the skeleton to crumble back into a pile of jumbled bones. Just to be safe, you kick them into the swamp, and watch until they start to sink. You hurry on, but very soon the path vanishes and there's no way through the black, sucking mud. You've no choice but to retrace your steps back to the junction and take the other way. At least the bones don't shudder to life again as you walk past.

Gain 1 ABILITY point and turn to **51**.

318

"You saw no one?" snaps the General, his pale eyes narrowing. "You're quite sure?" He steps a little closer, his gaze never leaving your face.

"I was just coming down the stairs, sir," you stammer. "And the alarm sounded, sir. That's all."

Roll one dice and add it to your WITS level.

If your total is 4 or higher, turn to **345**.

If your total is 3 or lower, turn to **270**.

319

The orb doesn't know where you are, but that doesn't mean it's going to give up. It hovers in place, just outside the doorway. You look about the ruined building that you're hiding in. There's no other doorway, but the roof has collapsed and you might be able to climb away from the orb across the other buildings.

Roll one dice and add it to your WITS level.

If your total is 7 or higher, turn to **183**.

If your total is 6 or lower, turn to **196**.

320

Your eyes flick back and forth along the rubble-strewn streets as you try to plan the quickest way to reach the forge. Eventually you come up with a plan, and you fix the route in your mind. Now you know how to get there – you just need to worry about staying alive while you do it.

"*It was a fine place once,*" rumbles a deep voice in your head. "*It is sad that it has come to this. Perhaps you will be the one to restore it to its former glories, eh ringbearer?*" The Iron Smith falls silent again, and you are left alone with his crumbled city.

Gain 1 ABILITY point and turn to **71**.

321

The largest griefer smashes the others aside and claims the right to kill you. It chuckles throatily as it pads towards you, its fur matted with blood. The others lick their wounds and their lips, eyeing you hungrily.

"Dinner time!" giggles the leader of the pack as it bites your head clean off.

322

Without the compass, you rely on pure guesswork. Neither path has any tracks on it, although the path to the right has fewer bones.

To take the left-hand path, turn to **51**.

To take the right-hand path, turn to **300**.

323

The box clicks open and inside it you find a small bottle of brown liquid.

"Drink it," says the lady. "You have potential – I can always tell – and perhaps this medicine will help to unlock it."

You raise the bottle to your lips and drink it down in one gulp. It tastes like cinnamon and treacle, with a bitter afterglow that lingers in your mouth. As it flows through your body, you feel stronger and braver.

Gain 2 ABILITY points and turn to **339**.

324

You don't have time to think. Pursued by the clanging of the alarm, you spiral down the back stairs as fast as you can. There are 793 steps in this staircase – you know because you've counted them so many times on the way up. Ahead of you, a hobtoad guard stumbles out of her watch post, kicking over her stool as she rises. She's holding a chicken leg – the alarm has caught her in the middle of dinner.

"What's the ruckus?" she growls at you, fumbling for her truncheon.

To lie to the hobtoad about what's happening upstairs, turn to **165**.

To try to take advantage of her surprise and attack her with the stool, turn to **57**.

325

The griefers are squabbling amongst themselves so they take no notice as you carefully clamber over the side of the bridge and cling on to the underside. The climbing is fairly easy at first because there's plenty to hold onto down there, but as you get closer to the centre of the lava river the heat becomes intense. The lava bubbles and spits, sending blasts of oven-hot air across your skin. You think you can smell your boots cooking, and the metal you're holding onto is becoming so hot that it's hard to grip.

Roll one dice and add it to your STRENGTH level.

If your total is 8 or higher, turn to **186**.

If your total is 7 or lower, turn to **134**.

326

The snail overwhelms you and drags you towards its mouth. You slash desperately at its tentacles and manage to cut yourself free, but not before it takes a bite out of your thigh. You flee, limping, into the darkness of the corridor beyond, turning left, then right, then down a staircase, then up another... and before you know it you're completely lost.

Deduct 1 STRENGTH point and turn to **356**.

327

You sidle about the long room, quietly looking for a way out. The windows are all locked – and besides, you don't think you could climb out of any of them without being spotted, since hobtoads are guarding the room. The stuffed animals stare unblinkingly from the walls, watching your fruitless search. One of the stuffed squirrels has a particularly annoying smirk, and as you look at it you notice a little service hatch just beneath it. It's cleverly hidden in a wooden panel, and a small bell hangs beside it. You slide the hatch open a crack and find a space behind the wall with a rope hanging down into the darkness – you can't see where it ends up.

This must be some kind of food elevator, to bring meals up from the kitchen. You peer about – the hobtoads are looking the other way, so you slide the hatch open a little further and quickly climb inside, grabbing the rope. You're glad it's dark – you can't see how far you would fall if you slipped.

Roll one dice and add your STRENGTH and WITS levels.

If the total is 7 or higher, turn to **245**.

If the total is 6 or lower, turn to **171**.

328

With a stern expression, the officer begins to search you.

"Let's see what you're hiding, goblin," he mutters. His fingers deftly probe your pockets, and he soon discovers the ring. As he holds it up to the light, you watch his casual expression change to one of astonishment.

"Where... did you get this?" he stammers.

You answer truthfully, explaining how you stole it from Darkmoon and have brought it here to give to the rebels. His eyes gradually grow wider as he listens to your story. "Is it really as the prophecy foretold?" he says wonderingly, staring at the ring and seeming to forget for a moment that you're there. "Can a goblin really be the one sent to help us?" He brings out a stool for you to sit on, and asks you to wait. "I do apologise for the less than hearty welcome you received," he says, almost bowing as he shakes your hand. He dashes out of the tent, then returns a minute later puffing and panting.

"This is yours," he says, pressing the ring back into your hand. "I am to take you to the lady at once." As he hurries you along the crowded path towards the largest tent, it seems that news of your arrival has travelled fast – everyone is jostling and trying to get a look at you. The guards at the entrance of the tent are already holding the flaps open for you, as if you were an honoured guest or a famous hero.

Turn to **249**.

329

The last thing you see is the tree dragon's teeth as it opens its cavernous mouth wide and snaps it shut around your helpless body, leaving you in pieces on the ground. The ring ends up lying among the leaves on the forest floor, waiting for an unwary traveller to pick it up one day...

330

You try to tell your story, but your voice tails off as you stare in terror at the dragon's long white teeth, which are as sharp as carving knives, and the smouldering flames at the back of its throat. You can't get a word out.

"YOU BORE ME," growls the dragon. "GO AWAY." It takes a deep breath, and you dive out of the way as fire erupts from its jaws. As you tumble past it, the ferocious flames singe your back, but you manage to scamper off as it curls up and goes back to sleep.

Deduct 2 LIFE points and turn to **218**.

331

You creep across to the counter and grab a handful of crunchy bugs.

Roll one dice and add it to your SNEAK level.

If your total is 6 or higher, turn to **252**.

If your total is 5 or lower, turn to **8**.

332

With its head swaying slowly from side to side like a serpent, the tree dragon towers above you. Its neck coils back, until, without warning, it suddenly lunges down towards you, opening its mouth wide.

Roll one dice and add it to your SNEAK level.

If your total is 4 or higher, turn to **357**.

If your total is 3 or lower, turn to **329**.

333

The door flies open and a guard-ghoul barges through it backwards, carrying a pile of papers. It's staring at the documents so you catch it completely by surprise when you attack. Your new weapon feels like it was made for you, singing as it arcs through the air. But the ghoul recovers quickly and shoves you across the room. With a growl, it leaps towards you, eyes blazing with menace.

GUARD-GHOUL

Rounds: 5   Damage: 2

YOU

If you win, turn to **199**.

If you lose, turn to **31**.

334

You slash at the grasping tendrils that try to drag you down, then you skip out of reach of the fanged flowers. Soon streaks of orange sap spatter your green skin. Like a striking snake, the larger flower crunches its jaws around your leg. The bite burns hot and you shout in agony and claw the flower head away, ripping it in half. The plant shrinks away from you, but your leg is already growing numb as the poison takes hold.

Deduct 1 STRENGTH point and 2 LIFE points.

The other plants are more cautious now and they keep their

distance. You waste no time in pulling a few tubes out to make a rope. Slinging it over the side, you climb down the wall. It's an ankle-breaking drop, so you're pleased you didn't try to jump.

Turn to **302**.

335

Trying to ignore the disturbing chomping noises, you squeeze past the snail. You only breathe easy again once you're well away from its stink. The corridor branches here and you don't know which way to go.

"*This way?*" suggests Boggo. "*Always turn right, my dad used to say.*"

You turn right, and then right, and then right again. As well as slimy snail trails, there are more stairs, more corridors, and then a statue that you first saw five minutes ago: somehow you've looped round on yourself.

"*Maybe we should turn left now?*" says Boggo. "*That's what my mum used to recommend.*"

You glare wordlessly at the ghost and take his advice.

Turn to **356**.

336

The gallery is a long, sunlit room with pictures all over the walls. Every picture is a portrait of the Master, done in a variety of styles, and his eyes follow you around the room. You pass a picture of him holding a book of poetry, then riding a fire-breathing lion, then fighting a battle against some centaurs, then contemplating a skull. He always looks very pleased with himself.

There are two doors out of the room – one leads to the main stairs and the other to the kitchen stairs.

"*Hey!*" hisses Boggo. "*I think there's a secret door here!*" His head emerges from the wall. "*But I don't know how to get it open. It's something to do with these pictures – there are hidden buttons on them, see?*"

You look at the pictures in the section of wall that Boggo is indicating. You notice that a small button is hidden in some of their frames. Perhaps if you press the right ones, it will open the secret door?

"But which ones?" you mutter.

Boggo leans back through the wall, leaving only his wiggling legs visible. "*Wait, what's this?*" Boggo's legs slide downwards. "*There's a scrap of paper on the floor with a picture on it. Maybe Darkmoon dropped it when he came through...*"

His toes wiggle excitedly. "*Maybe it's a clue! Here, I'll tell you what it looks like. In the top part of the clue, he's wearing a hat with two feathers... In the middle part, his shirt is striped, and he's carrying something... I can't make out what it is... but it's in his RIGHT hand. In the bottom part of the clue, he's wearing calf-length boots.*"

"So, which buttons do we press?" you mutter.

Look at the pictures on the next page. If you can work out which three buttons you need to press, add their numbers up and turn to that entry.

If you can't work it out, you can carry on down the back stairs.

Turn to **129**.

You release the reins and for a moment you feel as though you're still flying as your momentum carries you forward. Then you plummet into the empty air as Iron Mane soars away. This confuses the magic firebolt, which slows as if it's unsure which of its two targets to follow. Meanwhile, the ground is rushing towards you much too fast. You're dropping straight down into the mass of enemy soldiers, whose helmets you can now see glinting in the sun – just a few more seconds and you'll smash right into them. The wind tears at your clothes as you start to scream. Staring back up at the sky, you see that the firebolt has turned and is knifing down towards you again, just as the ground is rushing up to meet your helpless body. You shut your eyes and wait for the end...

WHUMP! The air is driven from your lungs as you land on something solid... but it's not the ground. Daring to open your eyes again, you find yourself back astride Iron Mane, who has swooped down to save you just in time.

"*Now THAT was a ripsnorter!*" cackles Boggo.

Gasping, you grab the horse's metal mane as it surges away, near to the ground. It's skimming just above the speartips of the enemy army, and the firebolt doesn't have time to adjust. It explodes as it hits the ground and the blast tosses enemy soldiers into the air. Your flight has swept you over the army into the rear where the great war engines are positioned, and you can see that lizardfolk are loading another firebolt missile into a big machine that looks like a giant's crossbow.

"*We must destroy that device before it can fire again!*" shouts the Iron Smith.

If you have the GOLDEN ACORN, turn to **157**.

If you have the LUCK BLADE, turn to **11**.

If you have neither, turn to **86**.

338

You search the dusty crates and boxes. Inside one, you come across a set of silver cutlery. The knives are blunt, but the forks are pointy. You grab one – it's the best weapon you can find. As you turn to leave, a dark shape slinks out of the shadows and miaows. It's Jervis, the Master's favourite cat. Your heart sinks – although Jervis wears a golden collar, he's more like a panther than a house cat, and he has a nasty habit of eating goblins. As you back away, the beast snarls and pads closer, his yellow eyes glowing with menace.

Add the SILVER FORK to your LOG BOOK. You can use this as a weapon and you no longer need to subtract 1 from all your rolls in a fight.

If you want to attack the cat with the fork, turn to **139**.

If you want to run away, turn to **66**.

339

"Is there really nothing you can explain?" you say. "I'm so confused."

The old lady shakes her head. "Your ring has been a curse on our land for thousands of years. By the time my brother and I first heard of it most people thought it was just an old story. But my brother did not – he found the Night Ring and unlocked some of its power, and he has ruled in darkness and horror ever since."

"Wait. Your brother? You're talking about Darkmoon?" you splutter.

"I regret to say that I am," she says. "I'm his sister. Or I was… But come, we must set you on your path, and prepare for our own battle. Please hurry, and do not forget us – that is all I ask."

She leads you out into the crowd, and once again you can feel everyone looking at you. Many of their faces look suspicious and doubtful, and a bewildered hubbub is building all around you as the lady leads you down to the open area at the centre of the tents. The crowd gathers then falls silent as she climbs on top of a barrel and begins to speak.

Turn to **242**.

340

"You have surrendered too often to the evil power of the ring," says the minotaur. *"You have been unable to resist it, and now it threatens to consume you. Look…"* She weaves her hands in the air, casting a spell, and a ghostly mirror image of your body appears. It's made out of

shimmering threads of white light and floats above the steps, and as you look more closely you can see a grey shadow is spreading tendrils throughout your body.

"*Do you see how the curse lives within you?*" says the minotaur. "*I cannot allow you to pass. If your weak soul took control of the ring's full power, who knows what you would do. It is my duty to stop you here.*"

She raises her scythe and steps towards you, sweeping the blade in long arcs. She looks almost apologetic, but fiercely determined too. You're sure that one blow from her blade would slice you in half – but you wonder if your weapons can even touch the ghost.

"*No enemy is safe from the ringbearer,*" murmurs the Iron Smith. "*Strike her down!*"

MINOTAUR GHOST

Rounds: 4   Damage: 3

YOU

If you defeat the minotaur, turn to **241**.

If you lose, turn to **131**.

341

When you come to the aspen tree, the turning looks more like a goat track than a real path – you would never have taken this way without being told about it. You follow the track as it winds downhill into a small valley. There are more trees here and you relax a little, knowing that the bat-riders won't be able to spot you. Winding deeper into the valley, you hear the roar of a swift-flowing stream and glimpse white water through the trees. Eventually your track joins up with a real path, and you quicken your feet despite all the miles you've come. You know you're nearly there.

Turn to **276**.

342

Before you're even halfway through the web, a massive spider scuttles down from the darkness. It dances around you, clicking its hooked legs on the stones, then lunges in to attack.

GIANT SPIDER

Rounds: 3   Damage: 1

YOU

If you defeat the spider, turn to **77**.

If you lose, turn to **191**.

343

The soldier grabs the girl and uses her as a shield. "So you want to protect her do you?" he snarls, and prepares to cut her throat.

"No!" you shout and lunge forward. But you've fallen right into his trap, and the guard grins wide as he runs you through with his dagger.

As you lie dying in the mud, you watch the goblin girl running away, her feet splashing in the puddles.

344

The giant doors grind open to reveal a long, dark chamber. A single beam of pure white light falls through the gloom from high above, bathing an iron sarcophagus in a ghostly gleam. In the dimness behind, a huge metal horse with outstretched wings stands watching over the grave.

"*Do what you must do,*" says the voice of the Iron Smith in your head, and somehow you know what he means. You move through the darkness to the light and place one hand on the cold, black iron. Frost crackles like a glove around each of your fingers, but you ignore the freezing chill, reach into your pouch with your free hand, and take the ring.

"*Now is the time,*" growls the Smith. "*Put it on.*"

Taking a deep breath, you slip the ring onto your frost-covered finger and wait. For a long moment, nothing happens, then an ice-white figure rises silently from the sarcophagus. He's very tall, and his beard is longer than it was in the pictures.

"*Let us go to your battle then, ringbearer,*" says the Iron Smith. "*I fear it may be too late already, but we shall try. We shall travel on my trusty steed Iron Mane.*" He reaches down and picks you up as easily as if he were plucking a flower. He cradles you in his arms and breathes a frosty breath across your skin. You feel your aches and pains go numb and fade away.

Add 5 LIFE points.

Without saying another word, he places you on the back of the metal horse and vanishes inside the great iron beast. The next moment, Iron Mane lifts up with a mighty flap of its wings and a rusty screech, and you're clinging on with white knuckles as it flies up into the darkness, spiralling ever higher through hidden passages deep in the mountain, until you burst out into the daylight at great speed. Blinking in the late afternoon sun, you glimpse thousands of figures far beneath you – the battle has begun! A swarm of swift shapes is buzzing to your left – bat-riders! – and the horse dives towards them with the Iron Smith singing a battle song into the roaring wind.

If you have the DRAGON'S SCALE, turn to **239**.

If you don't, roll one dice and add your SNEAK level.

If the total is 9 or higher, turn to **269**.

If the total is 8 or lower, turn to **110**.

345

He looks at you, nods once, then swivels away to follow the lumbering guard-ghouls up the stairs. You lean back against the cold stone wall and feel your heart thundering in your chest – you can't quite believe you got away with that.

Gain 1 ABILITY point and turn to **256**.

346

You wander among the iron generals staring at each in turn, but you can't make sense of the Iron Smith's clues and he doesn't speak again.

"*We should get to the forge,*" says Boggo. "*Our friends up there might be in trouble by now.*" He points at the distant ceiling. Frustrated, you walk between the long rows of soldiers towards the bridge, wondering how they would sound if they came alive.

Turn to **180**.

347

You time your move perfectly, creeping up behind the armour and leaping past just as it makes its turn. Without waiting to see if it's noticed you, you hurry off across the marsh feeling pleased with yourself... until you hear the clanking sound getting louder again. Risking a brief glance behind you, you see the armour striding straight towards you. It's coming for you!

To run away from it, turn to **169**.

To stand and fight the armour, turn to **35**.

348

As you're crouched there in the open wondering what to do, the largest griefer raises its snout in the air and sniffs. "I... shmell... dinner!" it giggles in a strange high-pitched voice. They all suddenly turn towards you, their eyes wide with anticipation and their jaws dripping, then they charge.

Turn to **128**.

349

You stumble and dodge, staring at the flailing bear to try and find a weak spot to attack. But you've no idea how to stop something that already seems to be dead. You're about to reach for the ring when something enormous jumps over your head and smashes the bear to the ground. At first it's a mass of writhing branches, but soon it untangles itself into a dragon-shaped creature. The fight is brutal and short, and soon the bear lies dead. With supple grace, the tree dragon leans low over the corpse and begins to weep. Wherever its tears fall, wildflowers bloom and the dragon mourns until the bear's body is buried by a thick carpet of flowers.

"YOU WERE RIGHT TO FIGHT THE ROT," it says, turning to you. "A WISE AND GOOD DECISION."

It leans right over you so that one of its tears splashes on your head, and you feel new strength running through your body.

"NOW FOLLOW ME," it booms, striding off down the path.

Add 2 LIFE points and 1 ABILITY point and turn to **146**.

350

Marcox sniffs out your hiding place, and drags you out by your neck.

"You thought you could trick me?" he laughs in disbelief as he takes your life.

351

You haven't got very far before a hand clamps down on your shoulder.

"What's a goblin doing here, I wonder?" says a voice, then a quick punch drops you to the ground. You still have no idea who's captured you. Whoever it is now drags you to your feet and hauls you towards an olive-green tent that's guarded by soldiers. An officer with the widest moustache you've ever seen stands up as you approach.

"Caught a goblin nosing about sir," says your captor. "A spy, I reckon." The officer nods coldly.

"In there," he snaps, and shoves you into the tent.

Deduct 1 LIFE point and turn to **328**.

352

The air becomes hotter as you get closer to the lava rivers. You're passing the wreckage of an amphitheatre when a voice calls out to you from a tumbled arch.

"Ho! Ringbearer! Over here!"

To investigate the voice, turn to **115**.

To ignore the voice and carry on, turn to **39**.

353

You reach the top of the bank just as the first golden rays of light are creeping above a line of low hills far to the east. You're pretty sure those hills are where the entrance to Crow Cave is. But it still feels a long way off, especially when you stop to consider the two possible ways of getting there...

To your right stretches the flat, desolate swamp known as Battle Marsh. You spot a narrow track that twists between hummocks of grass until it disappears into the low fog that hangs over the mud. The track looks little-walked. You know that thirty years ago, Darkmoon's forces won a terrible battle here – your own grandfather fought that day, though he never spoke of what happened. Ever since the battle, the marsh has been home only to ghosts, and the ground has remained poisoned by the terrible magic that was unleashed.

But the road heading into the dark, thickly clustered trees to your left isn't very tempting either: you know of several goblins who have disappeared in Phantom Forest, and an old legend tells that a whole army once marched into the dim green gloom and never marched out. People say that the oldest trees can talk and that they don't take kindly to intruders.

From above, you hear a shrill call. You whirl around, scanning the sky, and glimpse a pair of bat-riders skimming along the river in the distance. You hope they're still too far away to spot you, but you suddenly feel very exposed here on the bank – especially as the sun is rising fast and the day is getting brighter. Both the gloomy forest and the foggy marsh will offer a good hiding place and a way to get to Crow Cave by evening, if you can stay alive – but which path to choose?

If you'd like to head into Phantom Forest, turn to **176**.

If you'd like to cross Battle Marsh, turn to **208**.

354

It's easy to creep around the humans because they're trying to get a fire lit and it clearly isn't going well. Once you're well out of sight, you sneak back onto the track and continue up the hill. There are fewer trees here, and you can't help feeling a little exposed, especially as you're nearing the crest of a ridge.

Turn to **34**.

355

You creep towards the dragon and raise your weapon. Your first blow bounces off its scales with a metallic *dink*, not even leaving a scratch. It opens one sleepy eye and looks at you with a curious expression.

"NOW WHY IN THE WORLD WOULD YOU DECIDE TO DO THAT, I WONDER?" it booms, before opening its jaws and gobbling you down in a single bite.

356

Ahead of you, you see dim light spilling onto the stone slabs from an open door. You sneak closer and slowly inch your head around the doorframe. In the room beyond, five bone-white skeletons are sitting at a table, as if they were a family eating a meal. There are even plates and glasses set before them, although they are thick with dust.

"What happened here, Boggo?" you say.

"*Whatever it was, it wasn't good,*" replies Boggo. "*They didn't even have time to get up...*" You shudder and walk on down the corridor. There are doors everywhere now, and when you push them open you look into furnished rooms full of ancient dust. To your relief you see no more skeletons – but you don't see an obvious way out either.

You're aware that time is ticking away, and from somewhere up above you can hear that roaring again. *"Looks like this was a nice place once,"* says Boggo. *"Shame about the angry snails that moved in."*

"Yeah," you say, kicking at the slime on the ground. "They really like a mess, don't they? They leave their trail wherever they go."

"There's an idea," says Boggo, his face lighting up with glee. *"Maybe if we follow the trails we'll find the way out?"*

"Maybe," you say, thinking hard. "Or maybe they'll lead us back to their nest..."

Roll one dice and add your WITS level.

If the total is 8 or higher, turn to **172**.

If the total is 7 or lower, turn to **200**.

357

You dive out of the way of the gaping wooden jaws, feeling the heat of the tree dragon's breath as it passes over your back.

"Please! I'm sorry. I mean no harm," you shout. You know you won't survive another attack.

Turn to **25**.

STEP-BY-STEP COMBAT EXAMPLE

In this example, you have been found sneaking apples by a cook in the Tower kitchen. Obviously, they usually wouldn't come after you with a cleaver, but it's been a bad day and it gives us a chance to learn the basics of combat.

ANGRY COOK

Rounds: 5   Damage: 2

YOU

You have 9 Life points, so **before you start**, you cross out three of the hearts to make nine.

Round one

You choose 9+ and roll a 7. Your attack was unsuccessful. The cook inflicts 2 Life points of damage on you. Cross them off!

ANGRY COOK

Rounds: 5   Damage: 2

YOU

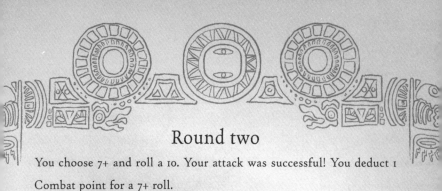

Round two

You choose 7+ and roll a 10. Your attack was successful! You deduct 1 Combat point for a 7+ roll.

ANGRY COOK

Rounds: 5   Damage: 2

YOU

Round three

You choose 9+ and roll a 5. Another unsuccessful attack! The cook inflicts 2 damage.

ANGRY COOK

Rounds: 5   Damage: 2

YOU

Round four

Things are looking nasty! With only two rounds left, you take a risk and roll for 9+ again. This time, you roll a 9. Your attack was successful! You deduct 3 Combat points for a 9+ roll. The cook lies defeated in a pile of his own pastry, and you can turn to the Victory entry.

ANGRY COOK

Rounds: 5   Damage: 2

YOU